THE
Area
FILES
51
THE BIG FLUSH

THE Area 51 FILES
THE BIG FLUSH

JULIE BUXBAUM

Illustrations by **LAVANYA NAIDU**

DELACORTE PRESS

Text copyright © 2023 by Julie Buxbaum
Cover art and interior illustrations
copyright © 2023 by Lavanya Naidu
All rights reserved. Published in the United States by Delacorte Press, an imprint of Random House Children's Books, a division of Penguin Random House LLC, New York.

Delacorte Press is a registered trademark and the colophon is a trademark of Penguin Random House LLC.

Visit us on the Web! rhcbooks.com

Educators and librarians, for a variety of teaching tools, visit us at RHTeachersLibrarians.com

Library of Congress Cataloging-in-Publication Data
is available upon request.
ISBN 978-0-593-42950-1 (hardcover)—ISBN 978-0-593-42951-8 (lib. bdg.)—ISBN 978-0-593-42952-5 (ebook)

The text of this book is set in 12.25-point Sabon.
Interior design by Michelle Cunningham

Printed in the United States of America
10 9 8 7 6 5 4 3 2 1
First Edition

For Jamesy, the best nephew
in the multiverse
—J.B.

To Anya and Anvika, love you
to infinity and beyond!
—L.N.

· · · CHAPTER ONE · · ·

HOLY CANNOLI

MY LIFE USED TO BE PRETTY SIMPLE. I LIVED WITH MY grandmother in a small cottage in a small town in the big state of California, and I attended Yawn Middle School, where the most interesting thing that happened was . . . well, nothing.

Nothing interesting ever happened at Yawn Middle.

Zero. Zilch. Nada.

I mean, there was that one time when Sarah Flore staple-gunned her fingers together, and for years after everyone called her Sarah Flore-Fingers. But I wouldn't call that interesting. I'd call that an example of how bad the kids at Yawn Middle were at nicknames. (You couldn't pay me enough to tell you what the other kids called me when I went there.)

Now I live with my Uncle Anish in the middle of the Nevada desert and go to Area 51 Middle School.

Doesn't sound like that big of a change, right? It turns out, though, my new life has been full of surprises. Things have gotten very weird since I moved to Area 51. Or more accurately, *because* I moved to Area 51.

RECENT SURPRISES!

1. My uncle, who I thought was a paleontologist in South America, is actually the head of the FBAI! (That's the Federal Bureau of Alien Investigations!)

2. The rumors about Area 51 do not do it justice. Have I mentioned it is filled with lots and lots of aliens? (But they call themselves "Break Throughs" here.)

3. My new best friend, Elvis, happens to be an alien from the planet Galzoria.

ELVIS

PICKLES

We're also besties!

SPIKE

4. Yesterday, Area 51 threw an epic Break Through—human dance party! That never happened at Yawn Middle!

And despite all these surprises, despite the strangeness of my brave new world, I am still absolutely shocked when I find myself standing outside my new school right before first period is about to start, watching as the sky unzips.

Turns out things can always get weirder in Area 51.

Because here is what just happened:

First we heard a bizarre sucking sound, and the air above me hollowed out like it was being suctioned out. Something tornado-like, but more solid, descended to the ground right in front of us.

Under any other circumstances, that would have been terrifying.

But this is Area 51.

I'm starting to get used to the otherworldly.

So instead of being scared, I felt my heart gallop in excitement. I was about to experience *my very first UFO landing*!

What I hadn't anticipated, though, was Elvis saying . . . "Mommy?"

See, I've only known him for a few weeks, but we've managed to pack a lot into our time together. With the help of our enemy-turned-friend Zane, we solved the mystery of the missing Zdstrammars. In the process, we broke in to FBAI headquarters and broke more than one Area 51 law, but I'm really not supposed to talk about that.

(If you ask, I'll plead the Fifth. If you don't know what that means, ask your parents. They might tell you. They might also plead the Fifth.)

We also ate lots and lots of pizza with Pickles and Spike.

And I've met Elvis's adoptive parents, Lauren and Michael.

I've learned a lot about Elvis since we met. Like I mentioned, he's a shape-shifting alien from the planet Galzoria, which is 63 billion miles away. Because his natural form is eight-dimensional with oozing edges, a shape beyond the limitations of human imagination, his appearance changes based on who is looking at him and how he makes them feel.

But maybe most importantly of all? Since we've become best friends, I've learned that Elvis is an orphan just like me. My parents died in a car accident when I was a baby. His parents died seven years

ORPHAN:
One big thing we had in common!

HUMAN

GALZORIAN

ago when they attempted to break through Earth's atmosphere to reach Area 51.

So why did Elvis run up to the aliens who have just parachuted out of a spaceship and yell, "Mommy?" Who does he see?

Here's what I see: two Break Throughs who look like friendly T. rexes going on vacation. Yup, Area 51 just got weirder. *Again.* They have tiny hands and huge heads, and they're wearing equally giant smiles. They look simultaneously thrilled to be here and the tiniest bit confused.

Before I can stop him—What if these Break Throughs are dangerous? Also, shouldn't we get to class?—Elvis runs up and throws his arms around the T. rex in sunglasses.

WHAT I SEE

I'm about to run after him, when I feel Uncle Anish's hand on my shoulder.

"Let him go," Uncle Anish says, stooping down to whisper in my ear. "I don't know what you see, but those two Galzoria must be Elvis's parents."

"I see two T. rexes who look like lost tourists," I say, and then marvel at how much my life has changed in such a short period of time. I'm staring at two ginormous dinosaurs—*DINOSAURS*—and only freaking out a little. And my freaking out has nothing to do with their looking like they could gobble me up in one friendly bite. Or that I'm going to be late for first period. (I *hate* being late.)

I'm freaking out because we all thought my alien best friend's parents were *dead*. Dinosaurs, shminosaurs. Class, shmass.

"Really, T. rexes?" Uncle Anish says. "I see two human-sized hawks. They're wearing Doc Martens."

WHAT UNCLE ANISH SEES

"Huh," I say, because I don't know how to respond to that.

Tears are streaming down Elvis's face now as the mom T. rex takes his head and crushes it to her chest with her tiny hands. The dad T. rex encircles them both with his large, scaled tail. This must be what a Galzorian family hug looks like.

Uncle Anish and I stand about fifteen feet away, not touching, because my uncle and I are not the type of family that hugs on the regular. But we're still close enough to feel all their emotions, as thick as the dust their spaceship kicked up. (And we're far enough away that I won't get knocked over by one of their prehistoric appendages.)

I get hit with a pang of jealousy, and then I feel ashamed of that pang. I know my parents will never descend from the sky in a spacecraft and surprise me on a random Tuesday afternoon, no matter how much I wish they would.

I shake the feeling away. My heart bursts with joy for my best friend and his family.

This is the stuff orphan dreams are made of.

Then the spacecraft door opens again, and this time my jaw drops. For real. Holy cannoli!

CHAPTER TWO

MINI-ELVIS HAS LEFT THE SPACESHIP

OF COURSE, THE TWO T. REXES WHO ARE ELVIS'S LONG-LOST parents are just the tip of the iceberg. Because not five seconds later, the spaceship door opens again, and a boy who looks exactly like Elvis, just much, much smaller and a thousand times more adorable and wearing a T-shirt with Elvis's face on it, walks down the ramp. A baby blanket trails behind him.

Is that . . . ?

Elvis looks back at me wide-eyed. He mouths the words *I have a brother?*

Hi, I'm Mini-Elvis!

Tiny T. rex jazz hands

I shrug, making wide eyes right back. I'm an only child. I can't imagine what Elvis must be feeling right now. I move closer to him, to show him that I have his back and I'm here for him no matter how complicated things get.

Mini-Elvis runs toward us, but just as he gets to the bottom, he trips over his baby blanket and face-plants at Elvis's feet.

"Oh my snoogles," Elvis says. He reaches out his hand and helps Mini-Elvis stand up. I look more closely at his brother's face. It's eerie how much he looks like Elvis. Same spiky hair and goofy grin. The only difference, other than his size, is that he's missing his two front teeth.

Man, this kid is cute.

"Elvis!" Mini-Elvis exclaims, and throws his arms around a startled Elvis's neck. "Meeeeeeeep! It's really you!"

"Um, hi," Elvis says, obviously overwhelmed. And who could blame him? It's not every day your dead parents and the brother you didn't know you had randomly descend from the sky.

And one of them falls at your feet.

And then tackle-hugs you.

"Hi, I'm Sky," I say, introducing myself to break the awkward tension.

"I'm Mini-Elvis. It's a pleasure to make your acquaintance, Sky. You're my very first Earthling friend," Mini-Elvis says with a lisp, and throws himself into my arms for a hug.

"Quick question: Why did your parents use parachutes and you didn't?" I ask. Elvis shoots me a look that basically says *This is what you most want to know right now?*

"Ugh, my parents love to make an entrance. They are so dramatic," Mini-Elvis says, and rolls his eyes. I look over his shoulder and see the two dinosaurs flossing. I guess he's right. They are apparently not only a hugging family, but a dancing one too. (Though let's be honest: they're light-years behind on dance trends. Who even flosses anymore?) I wonder if Uncle Anish feels the same way about dancing as he does about joking: that is, he never learned how.

"How old are you?" I ask.

"In Earth-years? Five. But I've seen some things," he says.

"Huh?" I ask.

"You know. I've been around the universe a time or two. I might be Earth five, but I'm a mature five," Mini-Elvis says.

I elbow Elvis, but he doesn't speak. He stares at his little brother, his eyes still big and round. Watery.

He rubs his hands over his head and then does the same to Mini-Elvis, as if to see if they are a perfect match.

"You must be wondering what we are doing here," Mini-Elvis says.

"Um, yeah, I guess you could say that," Elvis says, and I almost laugh at how flustered he looks.

"I did say that," Mini-Elvis says.

"Right," I say, remembering how literal the Galzoria can be sometimes.

CHAPTER THREE

AREA 51 IS
IN DANGER!

"PLEASE SAY THAT AGAIN, MORE SLOWLY THIS TIME," UNCLE Anish says. We are sitting in Elvis's backyard eating a Code 61156 (that's the code for drone-delivered Hawaiian pizza) to celebrate this very strange family reunion. Lauren and Michael (Elvis's adoptive parents) and Zane and his stepdad, Agent Fartz, met up with us here after school.

We're bundled up in jackets since it can get cold at night in the desert. We have no trees here to break the wind, though you'd think Agent Fartz would be able to do that for us. (See what I did there? Fartz? *Break wind?*)

"Well, it's exactly what we told you. Area 51 is in danger," Elvis's mother says. "I'm so glad we landed here and not at the other base, because that would have made our mission impossible. Wooo-weee, that portal is very powerful."

Her mention of the other base—aka Area 52—makes my ears prick up. According to Uncle Anish, we don't know much about it, except that it's the only other place Break Throughs can successfully land on Earth. On the rare occasions it's mentioned here, it always comes with a hint of disbelief, like no one is fully convinced it actually exists. Sort of the way I talk about narwhals.

Those can't be real!

Also, I assumed Mini-Elvis was joking about the certain destruction thing. Apparently not!

"You are all in like super-serious danger," Elvis's father adds. "By the way, does anyone have a wipe? Pizza from a drone feels very germy."

Mini-Elvis covers his mouth with his hands and whispers to me, "My dad is a total germ freak. Anytime anyone sneezes, he likes to shower, but I'm not sure he fits into any showers here on Earth."

"So you're not here to see me?" Elvis asks his parents, and all of a sudden his mood shifts. He looks sad and hurt, like he's been sucker punched in the stomach. "I thought you had died when I came here. That you couldn't survive the transition to the

Earth's atmosphere. I can't believe you're alive! And now you're suddenly here acting like it's no big deal? I don't understand."

I take Elvis's hand, give it a little squeeze.

"Yes, well, you're right," Elvis's mom says. "It was a close call. The ship wouldn't recalibrate to gravitational forces, so we had to turn around and head back to Galzoria after we dropped you off." Her dinosaur eyes fill with tears. "It was the worst day of my life . . . though I guess it would have been even worse had we actually died."

Elvis's dad chimes in. "And of course we're here to see you now, Elvis. We've been trying to come back to Earth for the last seven human years, but we weren't allowed until there was a mission sanctioned by the Galzorian government. Which is why we're here now to save your life. *All* of your lives." He spreads his tiny T. rex hands to include the whole table. "Also, we really needed a vacation."

"I don't know what your plan is, but we hope you stay here with us in our house until we find you more permanent accommodations," Lauren offers. I raise my eyebrows. I love Elvis's house, but like Uncle Anish's, it's not very big. I'm not sure two T. rexes can comfortably fit inside, not to mention sleep there. Things are getting cozy fast.

"Sure, sure," Elvis's dad says while he holds up his fork, as if inspecting it for cleanliness.

"Of course," Elvis's mom says. "Thank you."

Before I can ask any questions about the seemingly impossible logistics of this, though, Elvis's dinosaur parents let out bloodcurdling screams.

CHAPTER FOUR

AN EVEN MORE TERRIFYING SPECIES

DINOSAUR SCREAMING IS AS LOUD AND AS TERRIFYING AS you would imagine. The two of them let out roars so high-pitched it felt like a thousand teachers were scratching their nails down a chalkboard all at once. This is some Jurassic Park–level stuff. I shiver, then drop to the ground to take cover under the table.

"What? What is it?" Uncle Anish jumps to his feet and immediately grabs for the weapon-like thingy he keeps on his belt. This is why he is an FBAI agent and I am not. I hide. He takes charge.

"That!" Elvis's mom says, pointing at a . . .

Wait. It can't be.

Is she pointing at a teeny, tiny ladybug?

These massive dino-saurs are afraid of a *ladybug*???

Aww, she's so cute!

"The ladybug?" Lauren asks, still holding her hands over her ears. I'm pretty sure Elvis's parents have permanently damaged our hearing. I start to crawl out from under the table, where Elvis, Zane, and even Agent Fartz have also taken cover. "That's why you're screaming?"

"What is that terrifying species?" Elvis's dad says, lifting his disproportionately small hand to smack it.

"Nooo! Don't!" Now it's Elvis's turn to yell, though his yelling doesn't wake up every child in the state of Nevada, like I imagine the dino parents' screams did. "It won't hurt you. I promise."

"Oh! Oh! Is that Coccinellidae? A kind of small beetle, right?" Mini-Elvis asks as he whips a magnifying glass out of his pocket. "I've always wanted to see one of those. Look at its distinct markings. It reminds me of a tiny Polkydottamius!"

I scratch my head and look at Elvis, but clearly he has no idea what a Polkydottamius is either.

"Sorry. We were just startled," Elvis's mom says, smiling weakly at Lauren. She offers her tiny jazz hands in apology. "Anyhow, I just want to say—"

But before she can finish talking, Mini-Elvis sneezes. And then sneezes again. And again. I count seven in total.

Elvis's father looks horrified and quickly jumps up from the table.

Make that eight sneezes.

"Don't worry, honey. I'm looking for the disinfecting spray," Elvis's mother says, and starts fishing around in a giant handbag. "Hold on, where did I put it, again?" She seems to lose a lot of things a lot. Earlier she spent ten minutes looking for the glasses she was wearing, and there was another pair hanging around her neck. "This isn't good."

"What isn't good?" Uncle Anish asks.

"Can't you see? My darling Mini-Elvis is allergic to hedgehogs," Elvis's mom says, and throws her arm around her youngest son. I see Elvis wince. He's still awkward around her; this must all be weird for him.

"I'm allergic to a variety of species. I can't go within two feet of a Retinaya. Or a Splat. And human hair makes me itchy. Also, I throw up if I eat waffle fries," Mini-Elvis announces to the table.

"That's too bad," Elvis says. "Because Waffle Fries Only is the best restaurant in all of Area 51."

"And you're not going to believe this, but they only have . . . ," Lauren starts.

"Waffle fries," Michael finishes. The two of them laugh, but their laugh feels a little forced. Michael kisses Lauren's cheek. Now that I think about it, I'd bet this whole thing is tricky for them, too.

"Did you know that Waffle Fries Only is the only golf-cart drive-through fast-food restaurant in the entire universe?" Mini-Elvis asks. "Not just this galaxy but the whole *universe*?"

"Obviously, we'll keep Spike away from Mini-Elvis," Uncle Anish says when Mini-Elvis sneezes (number nine) and Elvis's mom again frantically looks for the disinfecting spray. Which is in her left hand.

"Umm, excuse me, but I feel like we are still missing the point," Agent Fartz says.

"And what's the point, dear?" Elvis's mom asks.

"The imminent destruction of Area 51!" Agent Fartz explodes—from his mouth, not his butt. Sorry, the Fartz jokes write themselves! Middle school must have been miserable for that guy.

A 13.785% CHANCE OF SURVIVAL

"OKAY, SO WHAT YOU'RE SAYING IS . . . WE'RE ALL GOING to die?" Zane asks. He sounds eerily calm. When I first met Zane, I assumed he was a bully. Turns out he's just bighearted and often misunderstood.

"No! Of course not," Dino-Mom (which is what I've started calling her in my head) says.

"Don't be ridiculous," Dino-Dad says.

"Then what are you saying?" I ask.

"You have to figure out a way to stop the space junk!" Dino-Dad says.

"We've calculated that you have a 13.785 percent chance of survival," Dino-Dad continues.

"13.785 percent is not zero," Dino-Mom says.

"For example, I've calculated that I have a 7.2

What's space junk?

KEEP READING TO FIND OUT!

percent chance of contracting a human disease while I'm here, and I still came," Dino-Dad says. I can't believe dinosaurs are so good at math.

Then I remember they're not actually dinosaurs. They're Galzoria.

"This does mean that the residents of Area 51 have an 86.215 percent chance of, you know, not surviving," Mini-Elvis says. "Obvi."

"Thank you, Mini-Elvis. That's very helpful," Zane says sarcastically.

"Tell us more about the space junk," Elvis says.

"Right, so we intercepted communication indicating that Area 51 is in grave danger," Dino-Mom says. "That's what I wrote down, I think. 'Grave danger.'"

"Oh my snoogles," Elvis says, as frustrated as the rest of us. He throws his arms in the air. "We get that we are in grave danger! Now for Galzoria's sake, tell us: WHAT IS GOING ON?"

Dino-Dad sniffs. "Well, okay. The intercepted communication told us that someone in Area 51 is working with the Arthogus to launch space junk at the base. The plan is to annihilate Area 51 and everyone in it."

"Umm, *annihilate* means 'to completely destroy,'" Elvis whispers to me.

FAMILY NAME: Arthogus

DEFINING CHARACTERISTICS: Multitentacled with suction cups. Wants to colonize Earth.

LIFE SPAN: Unknown. Facts given upon arrival deemed unreliable.

POPULATION IN AREA 51: Extinct on Earth

HOSTILE OR FRIENDLY: Hostile

This book is interesting!

How'd he read it so fast? I'm still only on page 5!

"What is space junk, though?" Zane asks. "Is it like all that plastic stuff you get in birthday party gift bags flying around in space?"

"If only it was a bunch of Pop Its," Agent Fartz says. "Actually, there are thousands of abandoned pieces of space equipment circling our planet—dead satellites, rocket wings, paint chips, probes—and they travel at super-high speeds. If one were to hit Earth, it would have the same effect as a large bomb. This has been a problem for years. But we never considered that it could be used as a weapon."

"Exactly," Dino-Mom says. "The Arthogus have repurposed a lavatory from an old Russian rocket and plan to redirect it toward Area 51. If it lands here, it will be a disaster."

WHAT IS A "LAVATORY"?

It's a fancy word for a toilet!

"Can you believe they're using something so dirty?" Dino-Dad says. "Gross."

"So what you're saying is that we have a 86.215 percent chance of dying because of a . . . flying toilet?" I ask.

Killer Space Toilet!

That could wipe us all out!

· · · CHAPTER SIX · · ·

NO SUMMER VACATION AT AREA 51 MIDDLE

THE NEXT MORNING, WHEN UNCLE ANISH AND I EAT BREAKFAST, we do not talk about the imminent destruction of Area 51. Instead, we eat Cheerios without saying a word. Which is how it usually goes with us. Uncle Anish is the strong, silent type.

Elvis and I golf-cartpool to school (that's carpooling in our golf cart, which we're actually allowed to drive on base), and on the way, we drop off Mini-Elvis for his first day of kindergarten at Area 51 Elementary. Life goes on, despite the fact that it may not sometime soon.

"Now, don't be nervous," Elvis says, patting Mini-Elvis awkwardly on the shoulder as we walk him to the front door. "You'll do great."

"Oh, I know that," Mini-Elvis says, and grins. He's still carrying his little blanket, but today he's also wearing a blue backpack. He fits right in, of course. One of the best things about Area 51 is that *everyone*—no matter what species they are or planet they are from—fits in. It's hard not to when some of your classmates have wheels for feet or noses on their butts. "The only thing I'm nervous about is whether they'll let me do my field research while I'm here."

"Field research?" I ask, but Mini-Elvis doesn't answer.

Mini-Elvis has entered the building!

Once we get to Area 51 Middle, though, the fear creeps right back in. We need a plan to save Area 51, and fast. No way am I letting some space junk ruin my already semi-ruined summer, especially now that I've learned I won't be getting a summer break.

Have I mentioned that school is year-round here? Yeah, no one told me either until last week.

THERE'S NO SUMMER VACATION?!?!

On page 89387, it clearly states, "Area 51 schools shall run year-round."

Before we make it to the front door, Zane runs right up to us without even saying good morning.

"Can you sneak out tonight?" he asks. "We need to go to Telescope Hill."

"What's Telescope Hill?" I ask. For a square patch of land, Area 51 is full of surprising nooks and crannies. Every time I feel like I might know my way around the whole place, I discover I haven't even seen a quarter of it.

"It's the highest spot on the entire base. It has these super-cutting-edge telescopes so you can see beyond our galaxy. My stepdad took me once for my birthday," Zane says. "It's mind-blowing."

Mind-blowing? We live with aliens. We've seen UFO landings (or in my case, *one* UFO landing). Occasionally, we puke because a Peeyou walks by smelling like microwaved diarrhea. For something to be considered "mind-blowing" here in 51, it must be truly out of this world.

Pun intended.

"We need to see if we can spot the killer space toilet," Zane says. "You can see everything from up there."

"Step one of our plan," I say thoughtfully, warming to the idea.

"What plan?" Zane asks.

"Our plan to save Area 51," I say. "Duh."

"Oooh, we need to get our wipe-it board," Zane says. "I love making plans on our wipe-it board."

"Later. But first Telescope Hill, wherever that is," I say.

"Telescope Hill is closed to the general Area 51 public, but agents can get permission for special access," Elvis says. "We'll have to come up with a way in."

"So should we ask my uncle or your parents, or maybe your grandma?" I look around the hallway to double-check that no one is eavesdropping. We're safe. A group of middle-schoolers are distracted with helping a Splat collect his Jell-O-like plasma.

Stop getting so jiggly with it.

"Are you kidding? We promised we'd stay out of trouble. No way any of them would say yes," Elvis says. This is true. Uncle Anish made it very clear we are not to do our own space junk investigation. *Or* tell anyone else what is happening.

"What are we going to do, then?" I ask.

"We're going to sneak in," Zane says confidently. He doesn't seem at all afraid of getting caught, maybe because he's so big and muscly. Which is weird for a twelve-year-old but occasionally comes in handy.

I surprise myself when I shiver at the idea. I'm always up for Zane and Elvis's rule-breaking semi-illegal shenanigans. That's half the reason I refuse to learn all the rules in the first place! Have I suddenly turned into a scaredy-cat?

Nope. It turns out Chill, a vapor alien who can walk through people, just happened to pass through me at that moment.

Once I shake him off, I'm one thousand percent game.

CHAPTER SEVEN

A TINY STITCH IN THE FABRIC OF THE UNIVERSE

WE DRESS IN BLACK HEAD TO TOE, PARTIALLY TO BLEND IN with the night but mostly because we want to feel super cool and spylike. If you're going to sneak out on a secret mission, might as well do it right.

It turns out Telescope Hill is almost exactly what it sounds like except it should be called *Telescopes* Hill, because there are four telescopes on the hill that form a square. By the time we reach the top— it's way too steep to take the golf cart up—we're all sweating and slowly peeling off our spy layers.

"Oh my snoogles," Elvis says, taking in the view. At this height, we can see all of Area 51 stretched out around us like a sparkly blanket.

"Holy cannoli," I say. Mini-Elvis, who sneakily followed us up, tugs at my sweatshirt. I look down at him; he looks so cute all spylike and dragging his baby blanket it's impossible to be mad at him for coming along uninvited.

"There's your home," he says, somehow able to identify Uncle Anish's house in the sprawling landscape. His house looks just like all the other houses, small and gingerbread-like from this height. It's funny to think of Elvis's home next door full of giant dinosaurs.

"Yeah, home," I say, tasting that word in my mouth. When I first got here, I never imagined that Area 51 could ever feel anything like *home;* at least, not like the cottage where I'd spent my whole life till then with Grandma. But I was wrong. I see Uncle Anish's little pink house, imagine the box of Cheerios in the cabinet and the tidy den, and think of Elvis, Lauren, Michael, and Pickles living right next door, and I feel warm and comfortable and cozy. *Home.*

"And there's mine," Mini-Elvis says, pointing up at the sky. "Sixty-three billion miles in that direction."

"Do you miss it?" I ask, squeezing his hand.

"Only all the time," he says.

"We need to divide and conquer," Zane says. "I'll take the first telescope, you take the second, Sky. Elvis, you take the third."

"Mini-E, stick by me. I don't want you to get hurt," Elvis says, all big-brotherly.

"Are you kidding? I'm not missing this," Mini-Elvis says.

"What are we looking for exactly?" I ask. I've never even heard of "space junk" until yesterday. Apparently, though, it's a known problem in our galaxy. There are even international organizations whose sole job is to track the abandoned space equipment circling our planet.

"A killer space toilet, obviously," Zane says. "When we get to the wipe-it board, I'm writing *find killer space toilet* at the top of our list."

"And what does a killer space toilet look like?" Elvis asks, putting his eye up to the eyepiece of the telescope. A second later he gasps. "Oh my snoogles! It is so beautiful."

"Do killer space toilets look like regular old toilets?" I ask, remembering how a few weeks ago Elvis, Zane, and I found ourselves hiding in a restroom at FBAI headquarters.

TWO WEEKS AGO

I step onto a metal stool and peep into the eye-piece of my telescope. The sky unfolds before me. Zane was right: it is mind-blowing. Since moving to Area 51, I've spent many nights staring up at the night sky and wondering about my place in the universe. I always get a slightly weirded-out feeling when I think about how small I am compared to its magnitude. But I've never seen anything like this. I'm looking at *space*. And not just space, as in the space that surrounds our planet, but space, as in a huge expanse.

The universe seems to go on . . . forever.

For the first time, when I think about how teeny-tiny I am, I don't feel lonely. Instead, I feel like I'm part of something. A tiny but integral stitch in the fabric of our infinite universe.

"Wait, I think I see something," Zane calls to us, and I reluctantly step away from the telescope. "Looks like a giant hulk of metal painted with a Russian flag."

But before I can make my way over to Zane, we're met with our worst-case scenario.

"PUT YOUR HANDS UP!" a voice through a megaphone calls to us, and my heart drops.

We've been caught.

· · · CHAPTER EIGHT · · ·

OGZ WASN'T BORN YESTERDAY

(but she was born three minutes late)

A WOMAN SHINES A FLASHLIGHT IN OUR FACES. SHE LOOKS exactly like Officer Glamcop, if Officer Glamcop cut her hair in a bob, wore glasses on a pearl chain, and traded in her police uniform for a cardigan. Getting random flashlights shined in our faces seems to happen a lot in 51.

"I can explain," I say, squinting at the woman who looks like Officer Glamcop but is not in fact Officer Glamcop.

"Step away from the telescopes," she says, and since she has the giant flashlight, which somehow gives her authority, we listen.

"Hi, OG2," Elvis says in

a friendly voice while he signals for Mini-Elvis to hide. Mini-Elvis ignores him, but it's adorable how quickly Elvis has slipped into his role as the older sibling. He's bossy. "Sky, this is Officer Glamcop's identical twin sister. She goes by OG2 around here."

"Hi," I say. "Wait, why are you the number two and not Officer Glamcop?"

Am I trying to distract her and make her forget that she just caught us sneaking into an off-limits part of Area 51? Maybe I am.

The question is: Will it work?

"Ugh, my sister was born three minutes before me. THREE MINUTES. Worst decision I ever made was not getting out of our mother's womb first. If I had, then I'd be Officer Glamcop and she'd be OG2," she says. Even though it's dark, I think I can see a tear glistening at the corner of her eyes.

"If you want me to call you something other than OG2, I'd be happy—" I begin, but she cuts me off.

"What are you kids doing up here?" OG2 asks, and I look to Elvis and Zane. How is it that we didn't come up with a plan for this beforehand? Maybe Zane is right: a wipe-it board would have changed everything. "And why is there a dog, a hedgehog, and a tiny dinosaur in a jacket over there?"

"Oh, that's my little brother. He's only five

Earth-years, and he's Galzorian. Strange that you see him as a dinosaur," Elvis says. I avoid eye contact with Elvis. I haven't told him I also see his parents as dinosaurs, because I'm not sure how you tell your best friend that his parents look like extinct oversized reptiles, even if he *is* an alien. Also, I'm not sure he'd understand that their little hands—so out of proportion to the rest of their body—totally weird me out.

Why are they so small?!?

"He's a cute dino! Wait, stop distracting me. I'm going to ask you again: What are you kids doing here? This area is off limits," OG2 says. "Someone better tell me what's going on. This is the second time tonight I've had to deal with visitors."

"Who was here before us?" I ask suspiciously.

"Ms. Spitz. She was setting up for the Fourth of July celebration," OG2 says, motioning to the tape on the ground and very clearly annoyed. "She's obsessed with maximizing the layout for everyone to watch the space parade."

"What's a space parade?" I whisper-ask Zane.

"I'll tell you later," Zane whispers back.

"Ms. Spitz had to put tape in the exact right spot. She even used a ruler! Now this place looks like a jigsaw puzzle," OG2 says.

"Ms. Spitz works at the Species Museum," Zane tells Mini-Elvis. "She knows pretty much everything about the universe. It's like talking to a book."

"She knows everything about the universe? I want to meet her," Mini-Elvis says. "I bet she could help me with my field research!"

"You kids are distracting me again! Why are you

here?" OG2 asks, and points at us with her flashlight for the second time.

"We're doing a school project on—" Zane says, but OG2 interrupts.

"Don't give me the old 'school project' excuse. I wasn't born yesterday," she says.

"But you *were* born three minutes late," Mini-Elvis says unhelpfully.

"Okay, okay," Zane says, still holding up his hands. Who knew flashlights wielded such a strange amount of power? "We were looking at the sky."

"Looking at the sky? Do you have any idea how much these instruments cost?" OG2 asks.

The word *instrument* automatically makes me think of music—of violins and pianos and the dreaded recorder I had to play in the spring concert at Yawn Middle—but then I realize she means the telescopes.

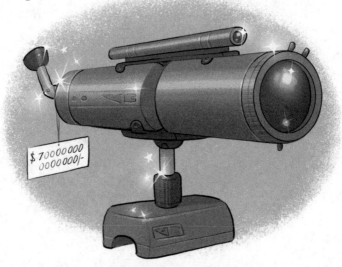

$ 70000000
0000000/-

"Holy cannoli," I say.

"Oh my snoogles," Elvis says.

"Exactly," OG2 says. "Which is why kids are not allowed to touch them. Got it?"

"Got it," we all say in unison. The thought of ruining a gazillion-dollar telescope is terrifying. Not as terrifying as a killer space toilet that leaves me with a 13.785 percent chance of survival, but pretty close.

"Sky, how's your uncle?" OG2 asks, suddenly friendly. It sounds like she's asking more than how Uncle Anish is. I have no idea what she's getting at.

"Fine," I say, shrugging.

"Tell him I say hi," she says, and smiles so big her glasses slip down her nose. She shimmies a little. Huh. Usually, when Uncle Anish's name comes up, people either cower in fear or scowl. "Now get out of here before I report you to the police."

And so we turn and run down the hill, no closer to saving Area 51 than we were a few hours ago.

CHAPTER NINE

BACK TO THE WIPE-IT BOARD

AFTER SCHOOL THE NEXT DAY, ZANE STANDS TRIUMPHANTLY in front of the wipe-it board in his house's hatch. All houses in Area 51 have hatches, which are like these special basement bunkers that have stocked refrigerators and locked doors. They're supposed to be for emergencies. My friends and I use them for brainstorming, because they have snacks. Lots and lots of snacks. Which is a necessity when you want to do some serious sleuthing.

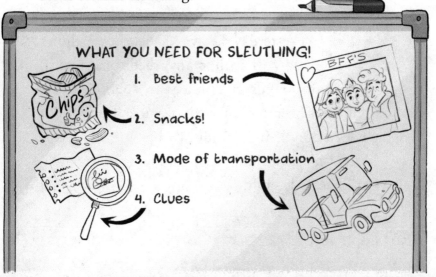

WHAT YOU NEED FOR SLEUTHING!

1. Best friends

2. Snacks!

3. Mode of transportation

4. Clues

"Okay, what do we know?" Elvis asks, and takes a bite of a Mars bar. *Of course* there are lots of Mars bars in 51. I bet they also have Milky Ways.

No one answers Elvis, because the answer is essentially *nothing*. We know nothing about what is happening.

Uncle Anish and Agent Fartz made us promise again last night that we wouldn't tell anyone what Elvis's parents told us, because otherwise there'll be mass panic. We were also told that we were not, under any circumstances, to get involved in this. (Let's just say we have a history of meddling in Area 51 mysteries.)

Spoiler alert: they get involved.

Zane writes SPACE JUNK? in all caps on the board with a marker.

"Did you know that there's a tiny art museum on the moon?" Mini-Elvis asks out of the blue. The kid likes to share facts and information. Yesterday he was shocked we didn't know that humans shed one and a half pounds of skin a year. "Seriously, the museum has been there since November 1969, and it includes a doodle from Andy Warhol.

"Art isn't space junk, though. Flying toilets are," Mini-Elvis adds sadly.

Zane writes *ART ≠ SPACE JUNK*.

"Okay, let's think," I say. "We know that the Arthogus are targeting Area 51, but we don't know how. Or when."

Zane writes *HOW AND WHEN*.

"We do know the *why,* I think," Zane says. "They're probably still upset about their banishment from Earth."

MY FAVORITE WARHOL

Andy Warhol is an American artist known for pop art.

Apparently, a few years ago, on July 4, there was an Arthogus uprising in Area 51. The Arthogus had plans to take control of 51, and then the rest of the United States, and finally all of Earth. In response, the other Break Throughs and humans of Area 51 banded together and sent the Arthogus back to their home planet. Since then, their old neighborhood has been left empty. It's super creepy. I don't recommend visiting.

"You know where we need to go?" Elvis asks, suddenly authoritative. "Astronaut Row."

"What's Astronaut Row?" I ask. First Telescope Hill and now Astronaut Row? How are there *still* parts of Area 51 that I have not only never seen but never even heard of?

No one answers me, because Elvis is too excited by the idea and Zane is too busy writing *ASTRONAUT ROW* on the wipe-it board.

"This is what I'm thinking: we need to talk to someone who understands space junk and the threat it poses," Elvis says.

"And if we can understand more about the weapon, maybe we can figure out how this all is supposed to go down," Zane says. The two boys smile at each other and high-five. We're getting good at being detectives. We're like the Scooby-Doo gang, but, you know, with an alien and a golf cart instead of the Mystery Machine.

It turns out Astronaut Row is on a small cul-de-sac on the east side of the base. The houses are well-kept and freshly painted with flower boxes under the windows. (Of course, in accordance with the "no plants" rule of Area 51, the flowers are fake. Still, they're pretty.)

"Why is it called Astronaut Row?" I ask from the front passenger side of the golf cart. Elvis is driving today, and I hold my hand out to feel the passing breeze. "Are the streets named after astronauts?"

Elvis laughs.

"It's where retired astronauts who have seen other life-forms go to live after their missions are over. They're routed to 51 so the secret of other intelligent life in the universe doesn't get out to the humans on Earth," Elvis says.

"What's in it for them?" Mini-Elvis asks. "Most Earthlings wouldn't move to Area 51 just because the government told them to. They'd require incentives, like money or a 401k."

I wonder if this tidbit about human behavior is part of the Galzorian kindergarten curriculum or if Mini-Elvis somehow has a database built into his central processing center. (The central processing center is what Galzoria call their brains.)

Guess I'll never know.

I have no idea what a 401k is. Maybe it's in the Area 51 handbook.

"Well, the astronauts get the best accommodations Area 51 has to offer, plus first dibs on all rations, and they get to continue studying the subject they love alongside Break Throughs," Zane explains, leaning between Elvis and me from the middle of the backseat. "Astronauts are usually obsessed with space."

"That makes sense. I wasn't even mildly interested in space until I moved to Area 51. And now I'm fascinated," I say.

"Before you came here, did you think there was intelligent life in the universe?" Elvis asks.

"Yeah, I think I did," I say. "The universe is too big for us humans to be the only ones out there, you know?"

"Anyway, we're going to see Nell Legswole," Elvis says. "She's been to Mars, and she's even lived on the International Space Station. That woman is a legend."

"Legswole. Where have I heard that name before?" I ask.

"You know Gertie from our class?" Elvis asks me.

"Of course," I say. "She's the best! I'd be failing Inkblit if it weren't for her. Also, she has a photographic memory!"

"Well, *her* last name is Legswole," Elvis says.

"Wait, we're going to see . . . Gertie's mom?" Zane asks, suddenly sounding very, very nervous.

Astronaut Row has the biggest houses on base. They seem taller and sturdier than the others, with wide

GERTIE

wooden slats and giant flagpoles that fly both the American and NASA flags.

"Not a bad place to retire," I say.

"According to the guidebook, the astronauts are not actually retired," Dino-Mom says, and I jump three feet in the air. Where did she come from? You'd think dinosaurs would stomp so loudly they wouldn't be able to sneak up on you. "They've just been repurposed."

"Hi! What are you doing here?" Elvis asks with a confused look.

"Just sightseeing," Dino-Dad says. "It's not every day you get to explore an Earth portal like Area 51. Hmm, this neighborhood is cleaner than some of the others."

Dino-Mom slips on a pair of glasses to get a better look around. I notice she has two more pairs on her head.

"By the way, Mini-Elvis," she says, "I scheduled a meeting with you and Ms. Spitz tomorrow to talk about your field research. Apparently, she's very knowledgeable."

"Cool," Mini-Elvis says.

"Well, we won't keep you, dears," Dino-Mom says, and smiles down at us before looking at her map. "According to this, the statue of Nell Legswole in Astronaut Square is a 'must-see'."

She does air quotes with her short fingers.

"It has four stars on PlanetAdvisor."

"Honey, get the camera ready!" Dino-Dad says.

"You have the camera," Dino-Mom says.

"It's in your hand," Dino-Dad says.

"Right, right. Toodles, kids!" And then the dinosaurs are off toward Astronaut Square. If we didn't have a base to save, I'd probably follow them. It's one more place in Area 51 I haven't visited!

· · · CHAPTER TEN · · ·

BIG GERTIE

THE WOMAN WHO OPENS THE DOOR LOOKS EXACTLY LIKE Gertie, except thirty years older and jacked like a superhero. She wears the same style of glasses Gertie wears and has the same ponytail and the same friendly grin. I wonder if she is also fluent in Inkblit, the grunting language of the Inkblotians. But unlike her daughter, Big Gertie has muscles in places I didn't know you could have muscles.

"Gertie," she yells over her shoulder, and as she opens the door, a delicious smell wafts over me. "You have some friends here to see you."

Mini-Elvis sniffs the air, and he makes a gurgling sound.

"What was that?" I ask.

"I was trying to approximate an Earthling's rumbling belly so she'd think I was hungry," Mini-Elvis explains. "There's food in there, and I want it."

"I made my famous inter-stellar banana bread," Nell says, and pats Mini-Elvis on the head like he's a small dog. Who knows? Maybe to her, he is. "Would you like some, sweet pea?"

"Sweet pea," Mini-Elvis repeats, and then, as if riffling through a list in his brain, nods. "Yes, *sweet pea*. An American term of endearment like *honey,* or *buddy,* or even, in some cases, *sweet potato*. Yes, please. I would love some."

"What are you all doing here?" Gertie asks, jogging up behind her mother, who has led us into the house and seated us on the living room couches. I've never seen Gertie outside of school, but she gives off the same warm and welcoming vibe here that she gives off in class. Like you can ask her a bunch of stupid questions and know she won't laugh at you.

Gertie's house is way homier than Uncle Anish's. The living room walls are painted light blue; one is covered with framed photos of Gertie's family and the other with kid art obviously done by young Gertie and her sister. The couch has the sort of sunken feel that makes you think a lot of tushies have clocked some good time vegging out here.

Uncle Anish doesn't veg. He doesn't *carrot* at all

for sitting. (Sorry, sorry. I'll see myself out. I know when I'm *beet*.)

Before we can answer Gertie, she starts talking again, a sly smile spreading across her face.

"You just saw me in school a few hours ago," Gertie says, looking directly at Zane. "You missed me that much, huh?"

Zane blushes.

"We came to talk to your mom, actually," Elvis says.

"But it's delightful to meet you," Mini-Elvis says, reaching out his hand for her to shake. Elvis smiles at his brother, impressed with his good manners. I want to tell her that we're here to see her, too, even though we're not, because I can imagine Gertie and me becoming real friends one day. Given my history of having *zero* friends in my pre-Area 51 life, that's a really big deal for me.

To be honest, Elvis is the first real friend I've ever had.

Zane is the second.

I sometimes worry that they might wake up one day and decide they don't like me so much anymore. That they'll become more like the kids at Yawn Middle and realize they never wanted to hang out with an orphan with a pet hedgehog in the first place. That I'll be left all alone again. I shake away the thought.

"So how can I help you kids?" Gertie's mom asks. Now that we're facing her, I realize we should have figured out before we showed up how we were going to handle this conversation without revealing classified information. We can't just say *So, Nell Legswole, please tell us everything you know about space junk and how it could possibly be used as a weapon to target Area 51 and kill everyone we know and love.*

Leave it to Mini-Elvis, kindergartner extraordinaire, to come up with a solution on the spot.

"Can we ask you some 'what if' questions? We don't want to reveal any secret intel," Mini-Elvis says. As much as I love his quick thinking, I groan inwardly at his use of the word *intel*. Zane and Mini-E really love spy words. *Info* works just fine, thank you very much.

"Sure," Nell says, smiling indulgently, like she thinks this interview is cute. She obviously thinks we have no "secret intel." "As long as it's about space, I'm your woman."

"It's about space. What can you tell us about space junk?" I ask. Nell has brought out her interstellar banana bread while we're talking and hands each of us a plate. If it tastes half as good as it smells,

61

this will be the best banana bread in the history of the universe. I spy with my little eye chocolate and melted caramel.

"Ha! One of my favorite topics. It's really too bad our space programs don't run on the same reduce, reuse, recycle programs we have here in 51. Instead, lots of countries' space programs—including ours—tend to abandon equipment when they're done with it, instead of safely returning it to Earth," Nell says.

"Why?" Elvis asks. "Wouldn't they want to clean up after themselves?"

"You'd think so, but it's super expensive to bring back old satellites or nonfunctional tech," Nell says. "The world's most elite astrobiologists lose a lot of sleep over this problem."

"So we just leave all that garbage out there?" I ask, horrified. "We're polluting not only our planet but our galaxy?!?!"

"Yup. Since governments won't take care of the problem, there have been some companies that have tried to find ways to clean up space. But so far they haven't found any good solutions," Nell says.

IDEAS TO CLEAN UP SPACE

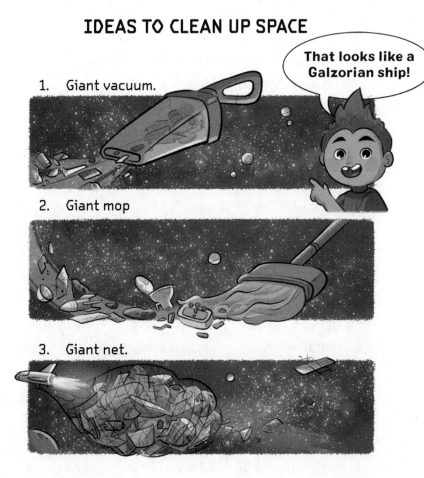

1. Giant vacuum.

That looks like a Galzorian ship!

2. Giant mop

3. Giant net.

"The most promising idea is using a giant magnet, but unfortunately, there aren't enough people who seem to care about space junk to make one,"

Nell says with a sigh, then takes a huge bite of her banana bread. Gertie echoes her sigh, as if she too is deeply worried about our polluted universe.

"I have another 'what if' for you," Elvis says. "What if someone wanted to target some place on Earth with space junk and use it sort of like a bomb? How would someone do that? Is it possible?"

"Huh, interesting question," Nell says. Gertie shoots me a horrified look, and I'm 95 percent sure she is asking me with her eyes: *Are we being targeted by a space junk bomb?!?!* I have no idea how she would know that, but I answer with widened eyes anyway: *Yup.*

I'm breaking the spirit of my promise to Uncle Anish, but I figure I can't get in trouble if I haven't said a single word out loud. Not even in Inkblit.

(By the way, you know that fake farting sound you make when you put your hand in your armpit? Do that four times and that's how you say "Yes, we're being targeted by space junk" in Inkblit.)

"It's entirely possible, but complicated," Nell says, deep in thought. "You'd need someone in space directing the junk, and you'd need someone on the ground who could give precise coordinates and transmit weather conditions. To make it work, they'd have to consider and then report back to space on a bunch of ever-changing factors—the wind, the sun rotation, the humidity, that sort of thing."

We must look confused, because then she says, "You know, like how we have ground control for rocket and airplane landings. If someone wanted to attack Earth from space, they'd need ground control here helping at the time of the attack."

This makes sense to me.

"And they'd likely want to do a test run with something smaller to make sure it worked. NASA does test runs all the time," Nell says. "You'd want to save your best equipment for the real thing."

"But if someone were to coordinate a big attack from the ground, there'd be no way they themselves could survive the blast," Nell says. "The best chance they'd have would be to take cover underground in a hatch, but then you wouldn't be able to direct the attack."

"That's not true," Gertie says. "What about if someone wore a special protective space suit, like the ones you used to wear on your missions, Mom?"

"Ah, you're absolutely right," Nell says. She smiles proudly at her daughter, and I see an echo of a look Elvis gave Mini-Elvis earlier today when he spouted some random and disgusting fact about toe fungus. It's a look my grandmother used to give me when I was polite to an adult or got straight As on my report card. I wonder if it's a look anyone will ever give me again now that my grandma and I are apart.

"We had these super-protective space suits that we wore at all times in case there was some sort of explosion or collision. They were awesome. I looked so cool in mine," Nell adds, her voice wistful.

Nell Legswole

"Ooh, can we see? Do you still have it?" I ask. I'm dying to see a space suit in real life, but I also want to know if they're easily available. Could anyone in Area 51 get ahold of this sort of equipment?

"I wish. We surrendered them whenever we landed," Nell says disappointedly. "It stinks, because they would have made amazing Halloween costumes for Gertie and Millie. Instead, every year we're forced to make costumes out of what we have at home. You know Area 51: reduce, reuse, recycle."

Hippie

Hot dog

Parking Enforcer

Office Worker

"If someone can't be ground control safely from here, would it be possible for someone on the International Space Station to do it?" Zane asks.

"No way. Not only are the astronauts who stay at ISS committed scientists who would never do anything to harm Earth, but it's also not scientifically possible. They don't have the correct tools or angles to direct a weapon from that far away. Too many variables they can't measure."

"Okay, one last 'what if' question," I ask. "What if someone were giving directions from the ground here in Area 51 to someone in space to target us? How would we stop them?" My voice shakes as I envision us all being flattened by a killer space toilet. That is *not* the way I want to go.

"I don't think you can," Nell says.

I look at Elvis, who looks at Mini-Elvis, who looks at Zane, who looks at Gertie, who looks at her mother. We are all thinking the same thing (except for maybe Nell): *We are so screwed.*

· · · CHAPTER ELEVEN · · ·
OCCAM'S RAZOR

TODAY IN "HUMAN EVOLUTION: WHY SO SLOW?" CLASS, we're doing a special lab project where we dissect human spleens. Let me say that again: *we are dissecting human spleens.*

I raise my hand. "Umm, Ms. Moleratty?" I desperately want to pretend to be sick so I can go to the nurse and avoid cutting open a fellow *human person's organs*. If I do that, though, I'm pretty sure the rest of the class will laugh at me. Already, Cubista has leaned over and said, "What's the big deal? It's only a spleen."

Only a spleen! I want to scream, and now that I think about that sentence, I realize it rhymes. My new motto for the day: *Only a spleen! I wanted to scream.*

"Yes, Sky," Ms. Moleratty answers, sighing. Ms. Moleratty is generally kind and interesting and a good teacher, though I sometimes get distracted wondering what she'd look like with whiskers. I should mention here that Ms. Moleratty is a human being, not a Break Through. Ms. Moleratty is *also* a human being who bears a close resemblance to a rodent.

HUMAN

Doppelgänger:
Someone who is an
unrelated look-alike
or double

RODENT

"Where do these spleens come from? I mean, who do . . . or did . . . they belong to?" I ask.

I decide that maybe knowing the origin of these body parts will make this all feel less gross. I have never understood how anyone could want to become a doctor—way too much blood and guts for me. When I go for my annual checkup, I've been known to cry if I have to get a shot.

Needles. Ick.

"They're from the Area 51 collection," Ms. Moleratty says, as if this is not the most disturbing thing anyone has ever said in the history of the entire world.

"There's an Area 51 human spleen collection?" I ask, even more horrified than I was three minutes earlier.

"No, don't be silly," she says, and I breathe a sigh of relief. "There's an Area 51 human *body parts* collection.

"When humans die in Area 51, they usually donate their bodies to science. When the scientists find they have no further use for the parts, they donate them to AFOUSD, the Area Fifty-One Unified School District. It's all part of our reduce, reuse, recycle program," Ms. Moleratty says, as if this is all totally normal. "We've found all sorts of creative uses for human remains."

AREA 51'S REDUCE, REUSE, RECYCLE PROGRAM FOR HUMAN REMAINS

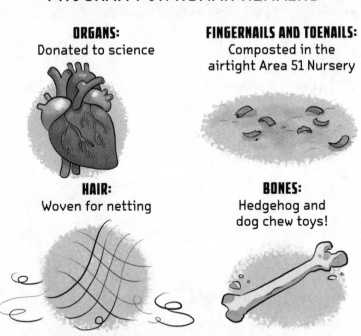

ORGANS:
Donated to science

FINGERNAILS AND TOENAILS:
Composted in the airtight Area 51 Nursery

HAIR:
Woven for netting

BONES:
Hedgehog and dog chew toys!

At Yawn Middle, we once dissected a frog in biology class, and it made me ribbit with nausea.

This, however, is peak disgusting. The formaldehyde smell alone is almost as bad as sitting next to a Peeyou. I wish this class had some Audiotooters, which is a species that farts out their ears and releases the delightful whiff of roses. Better yet, I wish I was Galzorian, like Elvis, and had no sense of smell at all.

"Don't worry," Zane whispers to me. "I'll do all the hard work, and we can talk to keep you distracted."

Before I know it, I'm chatting easily with Zane, totally ignoring the human blob of human guts laid open on the table in front of us humans. I am definitely not thinking about how every time Zane cuts into it, innards gush out and make a squishing sound. Nope, not thinking about that at all.

This is like the opposite of an ASMR video.

"Okay, so if Gertie's mom is right, how do you think our culprit is communicating with the Arthogus and doing ground control?" I ask, trying to keep my voice low. "It's not like you can mail a letter to space."

"Email?" Zane asks.

I start to laugh, then I actually think about it. "Could it be that simple?" I ask.

"Maybe," Zane says. "Occam's razor says we

should look for the simplest possible explanation first."

"Occam's what?" Elvis asks.

"It's not a literal razor," Gertie says, jumping into our conversation from the row behind us. "It's a problem-solving principle."

I don't know how much Gertie heard, but she's already been tipped off by our unexpected visit to her house yesterday. I trust her to keep this on the down-low.

"By the way, did you know that some planets get Wi-Fi?" Gertie says, and then takes her scalpel and slices right down the center of her spleen.

Not her own spleen, obviously. The one on the table.

"There was a giant router planted at the International Space Station," Gertie continues.

"Really?" I ask.

"Yup. Apparently, there was a big controversy about it in some galaxies. They banned social media—they realized way before we humans did that it causes anxiety and depression—but on some planets, aliens have a real addiction to those Netflix baking shows. The Cubistas love *Nailed It!*"

"There isn't internet here on base, though, other than at FBAI headquarters," Zane says.

"And police headquarters. I live right next door, so I've learned to hack into the signal," Gertie says. "Don't tell anyone, but I'm an expert hacker. Self-taught. I made myself a laptop out of recycled parts."

"So hypothetically speaking, if we needed your help hacking into the Area 51 police headquarters computer systems, you could hypothetically help us?" I ask.

"Hypothetically?" she says. "Abso-freaking-lutely."

· · · CHAPTER TWELVE · · ·
BEST-LAID PLANS

WE DRESS IN CAMO FOR OUR NEXT MISSION. THIS TIME, we have a new member on our team.

"Listen, this is the most fun I've had in months, so I'm not complaining, but are we doing this for the reasons I think we're doing this?" Gertie asks. "Because on a scale of one to ten in terms of freaked-out-ness, I'm kind of at a solid eight after what you asked my mom yesterday."

"We've been sworn to secrecy," Elvis says.

"Hmm," she says. "I think I need a little more information than that."

"We need to find out if anyone has been sending any emails off base," I say. "For, you know, *reasons*."

I get that same sense I have with Elvis and Zane, that I can communicate without having to say a word. Gertie nods at me. She gets it.

Maybe that means we're already friends.

"This is for all of our safety," Zane says, and clasps his hands behind his back dramatically. What is he doing? Is he . . . flexing?

"This job should be easy," Gertie says, ignoring whatever is happening with Zane. "You need special permission to use the internet here, so the system will have a record of anything sent."

"And you can just access that data?" Mini-Elvis asks. "Without special permission?"

"It should take about five minutes. I'll need to get set up with my laptop first, then access a computer at the police station, and you guys are going to have to cause a distraction so they don't see me hacking into their system. But yeah, easy-peasy," Gertie says. Zane looks at her, impressed, and his cheeks redden. I look at Gertie to see what he's staring at—maybe she has something on her face?—but nope, it's just the same old Gertie.

Since we need to come up with a distraction, we all shout out our ideas at once.

VARIOUS PLANS TO DISTRACT THE AREA 51 POLICE

ELVIS'S PLAN: Fake fainting in domino formation

SKY'S PLAN: Read out loud to the police officers from the Area 51 handbook so they all fall asleep

ZANE'S PLAN: Set off the Area 51 alarm system

SPIKE'S PLAN: Order lots and lots of pizzas

PICKLES'S PLAN: Get down on one knee and propose to Spike in the front of the police station

In the end, we don't go with any of these plans, because Gertie comes up with something way better.

CHAPTER THIRTEEN

IT'S FUN TO STAY AT THE YMCA

"WHAT IS A FLASH MOB EXACTLY?" ELVIS ASKS, WHEN GERTIE first suggests it.

"It's when a group of people get together and do a surprise performance together. Usually it's a cool dance or something, and then they leave like nothing happened," Gertie says.

"This is my first flash mob," I say.

"This is everyone's first flash mob," Elvis says.

Not mine!

We look in the golf cart glove compartment for some sort of music player, which according to Gertie is essential to our plan. Elvis claims that Uncle Anish keeps an old-timey musical device called a Walkman in there. We have no idea what it might hold—apparently Walkmen (or is the plural Walkmans?) can play only one album at a time from their weird two-holed tape thingies—but we're hoping that it's something we recognize.

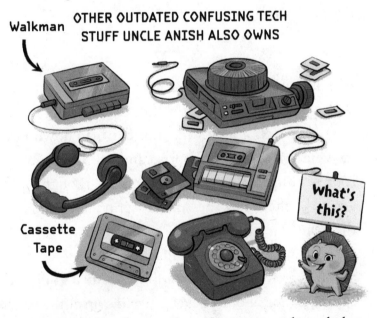

Walkman

OTHER OUTDATED CONFUSING TECH STUFF UNCLE ANISH ALSO OWNS

Cassette Tape

What's this?

We find the player, eject the tape, and read the label. It says *Village People,* which means absolutely nothing to us, so we put it back in and hit play. Nothing happens.

"Pull out the headphones," Gertie says, like we're the stupidest people she has ever met.

"Right," Zane says, blushing again, and as he pulls out the headphone cord that's been plugged into the device, he flexes his biceps.

Music starts blaring.

"Oooh, I know this one!" Zane exclaims happily.

"Everyone knows this one!" Elvis says.

"Even me," Mini-Elvis says. "They play it at parties on Galzoria all the time."

Five minutes later, we're set for our performance. We've practiced once in the golf cart parking lot of the police station, with the music turned down low so we don't spoil the surprise ambush. A Sanitizorian walking by did hear the music, though, and got so excited that she started spraying in time to the beat.

Now we all reek of disinfectant.

We enter the police station one at a time, all casual, hands in our pockets. We line up at the front of the main desk, Elvis hits play on the Walkman, and boom . . . we start our flash mob. True, the six of us are not quite a mob—we're more like a flash small, tight-knit group—but this will have to do.

"What is happening?" asks another Area 51 officer. He's short and stocky and has the gruff authoritative voice of a WWE wrestler.

"I think it's a . . . flash mob?" Officer Glamcop responds, though she too looks confused.

"I think it's a flash small, tight-knit group," says Officer Betty White, who is perhaps the oldest person in Area 51, from the back of the room. I thought she had retired after arresting Belcher and Roidrage (the guys who kidnapped the Zdstrammars), but I guess I was wrong. I'm happy to be. I get the feeling she's a legend here on base.

"I know this song," the WWE wrestler–looking officer says.

"Everyone knows this song," Officer Glamcop says.

"Join in," I say.

"It's fun to stay at the YMCA," we all sing, and continue our frantic dancing.

My heart beats fast, and I feel sweat bead at my temples. We're desperate to keep the eyes of all the police officers on us. It was way less nerve-racking when we only had an audience of one Sanitizorian, and, you know, our friend wasn't illegally hacking into the police network.

Out of the corner of my eye, I see Gertie slip into the station and behind a computer in the back of the room. This means she's made it to the second step of her plan. Will they see her? Will we get caught?

Somehow I feel like I've been dancing both forever and for only a few seconds. It doesn't seem like nearly enough time for Gertie to have worked her magic, but then again, Gertie is fluent in Inkblit and has a photographic memory. This could be a cinch for her.

The song comes to an end, and we stand there awkwardly. My arms are tired and we're all out of breath except Zane. Seriously, when does that kid fit in so much exercise?

I look at Mini-Elvis, who has been in charge of watching Gertie and reporting back, and he gives me a thumbs-up. Did she actually pull it off? I can't see her in the back of the room anymore. Where did she go?

"Well, that was fun," Office White says in her gravelly voice. She is a surprisingly good dancer. "I haven't heard that song since the Spotifies had a party."

The Spotifies are a species with built-in radios for "ears." They're phenomenal at soundtracks.

"Thanks for the break, kids," Officer Glamcop says. "By the way, I heard from my sister that you were sneaking around Telescope Hill."

"More like *Telescopes* Hill," the WWE wrestler–cop guy mutters under his breath.

"We were doing research for school, but we're sorry—we won't do it again," I say, determined to stick to my story.

"Your uncle told me that if we catch you guys doing any investigating we should report it to him immediately. And maybe throw you in handcuffs just to scare some sense into you," Officer Glamcop says, shaking her head, and then she surprises me by smiling. "I'm so glad I can report to him that you all are just being happy, silly kids. Look at you with your adorable flash mobs!"

"Right, we're just being happy, silly kids," Zane says so unnaturally that I'm sure we'll be arrested any second.

"Next time, let's do ABBA," Office Betty White says, and after we promise her a future "Dancing Queen" flash small, tight-knit group, we're off to find out what Gertie discovered.

CHAPTER FOURTEEN

WE GOT THE INTEL

GERTIE GRINS, AND I NOTICE SHE HAS TWO HUGE MATCHING dimples in her cheeks.

"Like I said: easy-peasy," she says, and holds up her laptop like it's a trophy.

Zane looks at Gertie with such admiration, you'd think she managed to break into a police station and hack into a highly encrypted system without getting caught.

Wait . . . she actually did.

We've gathered in Uncle Anish's hatch because Zane wasn't sure whether his parents had restocked their snacks, and he said the hatch was the perfect place to talk about our new intel.

I got all your info right here.

"How did you do it? By installing malware, cross-strangulating their frequency, and then spoofing the network?" Mini-Elvis asks. We all stare at him with our jaws dropped. Elvis clamps an arm around his little brother's shoulders proudly. "What? Hacking 101 is a required course in preschool on Galzoria."

Gertie nods.

"Yup, and I was able to download a list of everyone who sent messages in the last thirty days," she says. "I haven't read it yet, but my guess is that it's a short list, because you have to get special permission to communicate off base."

"Were you able to get the content of the messages?" I ask. "Can we see what people wrote?"

"Unfortunately not. I didn't have enough time. That's a much longer job. But at least we can see who's attempting to communicate outside 51," Gertie says. She presses a few buttons on her laptop and types a password so quickly that my vision blurs. Then she turns the screen toward us. There are only three names on the list.

1. Agent Anish Patel

2. Officer Glamcop

3. Agent Lauren Spalding

"Uncle Anish and Officer Glamcop make sense. They *have* to email off base to the people who know the Area 51 secret in Washington, DC," Zane says. "But . . ."

"My mom?" Elvis gasps.

"Your *adoptive* mom," Mini-Elvis corrects him, and Elvis shoots him a hurt look. Lauren *is* Elvis's mother (or, at the very least, *one* of his mothers), even if she didn't give birth to him. "Sorry. I didn't mean it pejoratively. I like accuracy."

"Pejorative" means expressing disapproval.

"Why would your mom be communicating off base?" I ask.

"I have no idea, but I'm going to find out," Elvis says.

CHAPTER FIFTEEN

A FAMILIAR SUSPECTS LIST

ZANE WRITES THE WORDS *AGENT LAUREN SPALDING* **AT THE** top of our suspects list. It looks scary in all caps on the wipe-it board.

"I can't believe my mom's name is there," Elvis says sadly.

"Don't worry. Your mom is an Area 51 legacy! She'd never do anything to hurt this place or anyone in it," I say. I know exactly how Elvis feels right now. When Uncle Anish was the number one suspect for the Zdstrammar kidnapping, I was equally devastated and worried. For a hot minute there, I even thought he might be guilty.

It's a scary feeling when you're not sure you can trust the person you need to trust most in the world.

"I know you're right," Elvis says, but he's nibbling on his bottom lip. "She loves 51!"

I TRUST YOU, SPIKE.

He speaks my love language: pizza!

"She does," Gertie says, and pats Elvis's hand. "Even I know that!"

"I only put her up there so we get to cross her off soon," Zane says. "We all know she's not involved with this."

"It's just that—" Elvis says, but Mini-Elvis cuts him off.

"You're being very human right now, Elvis," he says. I look over at him, confused.

"How?" I ask.

"He's jumping to conclusions! There are a million other plausible reasons for your mom to be sending an email. There's no need to go immediately to the worse one," Mini-Elvis adds. Not for the first time, I think about how wise he is for five years old. I could use a year in a Galzorian kindergarten. "Ms. Spitz, my new field research advisor, who everyone said knew everything about the universe, had to be corrected 2,465 times when we met the other day, because she kept leaping to conclusions based on very little evidence."

We ignore this aside, mostly because we don't want to get distracted by Mini-Elvis talking about his kindergarten field research, which is interesting but also way too complicated for this middle schooler. Yesterday, for no reason at all, he started explaining varying perceptions of time according to different species, and my brain started aching.

(Apparently, for the Splats, time is a circle. For the Peeyous, there is only what they call "the now." And Inklbit have no grunts or even symbols for the concept of time; to them, time is merely a human construct. Right? It's so confusing. I didn't understand it yesterday, which means I probably won't understand it tomorrow. Unless the Peeyous are right and there is no yesterday and there is no tomorrow. Yeah, I'm going to stop now or I'm going to have to lie down.)

"Maybe your mom's trying to buy you some awesome birthday present. When is your birthday, by the way?" I ask, trying to divert Elvis's attention from the stress. Too bad we've recently flash mobbed, because that's the sort of thing that would totally work on Elvis. Next time there's an emergency, we're definitely rocking out to ABBA.

"He doesn't have one," Mini-Elvis says. "We work on a different calendar in Galzoria. We think your concept of a birthday is kind of adorable—"

"October thirtieth," Elvis says, interrupting his little brother.

"YOU HAVE A BIRTHDAY?!" Mini-Elvis asks, sounding slightly hysterical.

Elvis shrugs.

"When I moved to Area 51, my mom and dad said I should get a day like everyone else, where we celebrate me. So we picked October thirtieth, the day I landed," he says.

"The day before Halloween," I say. "That suits you."

"Why?" Elvis asks, and he looks genuinely curious.

"You know, because of Halloween being about costumes, and you shapeshifting," I say.

"I want a birthday too, then," Mini-Elvis says. His whiny voice reminds me that despite his amazing central processing center, he's still only a little kid. He even stomps his foot.

"How about April first?" Zane asks, snickering a little, and Gertie glares at him. Zane's cheeks redden.

"Nice try. That's April Fool's Day," Mini-Elvis says. "We learn all Earth holidays on Galzoria in kindergarten, and subcategorize by continent and then country. We're tested the way you're tested on your multiplication tables, though we learn those in pre-preschool."

"How about June seventeenth?" I suggest randomly.

"National Eat Your Vegetables Day?!?!" Mini-Elvis looks thrilled. "Perfect!"

"My birthday is January fourteenth," Gertie

says, and I swear I see Zane make a mental note. "It's National Dress Up Your Pet Day."

"Listen, if any of us want to make it to our next

birthday, we have to stop the killer space toilet," I say, even though I'm definitely finding poor Spike a silly poop emoji costume for next January. "So let's get back to the mission."

Over the next hour, we start to formulate a new plan, and the wipe-it board slowly gets filled.

"My money is on Roidrage and Belcher," Zane

says as he munches on a Twizzler. "Did you know that part of their punishment for kidnapping the

Zdstrammars is to live in the run-down old Arthogus neighborhood?"

"Really? I guess that makes sense," I say. I've only driven my golf cart through that side of the base once. And for good reason. I was too scared to go back.

"Yeah, Roidrage and Belcher are supposed to clean it up. My stepdad said that's part of their punishment," Zane says.

"I heard they're constantly asking for yarn and no one knows why," Gertie says.

"Could they be using yarn to communicate with the Arthogus?" I ask.

"My Magic Eight-Ball says 'highly unlikely,'" Mini-Elvis says.

"Galzoria have Magic Eight-Balls?" Zane asks.

"No, I was trying out what you Earthlings call sarcasm. Did it work?" Mini-Elvis asks.

I shrug.

"The Arthogus clearly want revenge. And Belcher and Roidrage have a motive too," Elvis says, ignoring Mini-Elvis, which is a very big-brother thing to do, come to think of it. Elvis has been uncharacteristically quiet all day. I don't blame him. He has a lot on his mind, given the whole long-lost parents returned and the "Surprise! You have a little brother!" events of the last few days. Not to mention his mom's name is still in all caps on the wipe-it board.

"You think Roidrage and Belcher want to destroy 51?" I ask.

"I bet Roidrage and Belcher are still angry about your uncle and Officer Glamcop getting the jobs they wanted. And who would want to live in Arthogus housing? Not to mention Officer Roidrage has that weird Arthogus obsession," Elvis says. I remember how when I first met Officer Roidrage, I assumed his tattoo was just a bizarre octopus. Now I know better.

"But he hates the Arthogus," I say. "I thought he got his tattoo to remember fighting in the rebellion."

"What's the expression? 'The enemy of my enemy is my friend,'" Zane says.

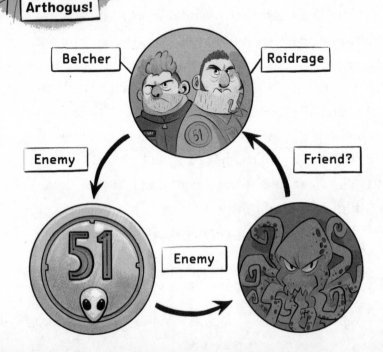

That's an Arthogus!

Belcher

Roidrage

Enemy

Friend?

51

Enemy

"I don't understand," I say.

"Maybe Belcher and Roidrage hate Area 51 even more than they hate the Arthogus, and teaming up with them means they can get revenge on us," Elvis says.

··· CHAPTER SIXTEEN ···

A GOLF CART
FULL OF LIARS

WE DECIDE THAT AFTER SCHOOL WE'LL TAKE A FIELD TRIP TO the other side of the base and see what's happening with Belcher and Roidrage. Of course, that means we need to lie to the adults. It occurs to us as we stand outside Elvis's house that we now have an extra set of parents to face down. The fact that these adults are literal dinosaurs (at least to me) somehow doesn't stop us.

"We have a research project for UFO history month," I told Uncle Anish when I asked to borrow his golf cart. The number one best thing about Area 51, besides my new best friends, is that I, Sky Patel-Baum, a twelve-year-old girl, can legally drive here. I mean that I can drive a golf cart, not an actual car, and I can't go more than twenty-five miles an hour, unless I push the secret super-charge button, which I've sworn never to touch. But still. I can drive! For real! The fastest thing I drove back home in California was nothing. I drove nothing in California, except maybe my grandmother bananas.

Uncle Anish asked me all sorts of follow-up questions about my research project: What UFO had I chosen to write about? Why had I chosen that one? How did I intend to research it? Would I be conducting any interviews? I answered easily, because the truth is I do have a research project to do for UFO history month. I just don't intend to do it *today*.

Elvis's parents are trickier. Lauren and Michael seem suspicious even before we tell them we're planning to go anywhere. The Dino-parents, who have moved into Elvis's tiny house, are even worse. Their spiky little teeth seem menacing. Like if they find out we're lying, they'll take a bite out of my leg.

"Take a walkie to be extra safe," Michael says, and tosses Elvis the walkie-talkie he keeps clipped to a belt loop on his jumpsuit.

"We're fine," Elvis says. "Why is everyone suddenly so overprotective? Is this because of the space junk? I doubt that's happening today."

"Actually, it's because last time we let you wander wherever you wanted, you ended up getting entangled in a kidnapping case," Lauren says.

"Kidnapping?" Elvis's dino-mom asks, horrified.

"Don't worry. We were never in any real danger," Elvis says, and for a second I think he's going to add *Mom* or *Mommy,* but he doesn't. Even language is tricky now that he's suddenly found himself with two mothers, when just a few days ago he thought he only had one. That's two more than I have, but to be honest, I'd only borrow Lauren as my mom if he was willing to share. I'm not sure how I'd adjust to being parented by a giant extinct prehistoric creature.

Anyhow, I'm not sure Elvis is telling the truth. When we were trying to find the missing Zdstrammars, it *definitely* felt like we were in real danger. At one point, I thought we'd find ourselves locked up in Area 51 jail, or worse, banished from base.

"Be home by eight. We're having a family dinner," Lauren says.

"Yes, be home by eight. We're having a family dinner," Dino-Mom echoes.

"With your Galzorian mom and dad," Michael says, choking on the words a little bit.

"Yes, with your Earthling relations too," Dino-Mom adds, which is . . . awkward. Like they are engaging in a secret parent battle.

"And make sure you wash your hands a lot," Dino-Dad says.

"Don't worry. We'll be back by eight," Elvis says.

CHAPTER SEVENTEEN

A RELAXING STAKEOUT

"WE'RE STARTING WITH A RECON MISSION," ZANE SAYS, ONCE he jumps into the golf cart. I'm driving, Elvis has the front seat, and Zane and Gertie are in the back. We start heading toward the Arthogus neighborhood.

"Hi!" Mini-Elvis says, popping up out of nowhere and scaring the spaghetti out of us. We all scream. Apparently, he snuck into the trunk of our golf cart with Spike and Pickles.

"Oh my snoogles, you almost gave me a heart attack," Elvis says.

"Physiologically speaking, Galzoria don't have hearts," Mini-Elvis says, and Elvis winces.

"We get to dissect human hearts in eighth grade," Zane says excitedly.

"No. Just no," I say. "Anyhow, what's a recon mission?"

Zane loves to show off with these fancy spy words, and I never know what he's talking about.

"*Recon* is short for *reconnaissance*," Mini-Elvis calls out from the back. "As in 'a mission to gather information.'"

"You sure you're five?" I ask him.

"I told you. I've been around the universe a few times," Mini-Elvis says.

"It means we're going on a stakeout," Zane says, and I groan.

"Here's the plan," Elvis says. "We're going to the outskirts of the Arthogus neighborhood to take a peek. See what's happening over there. That's it. We will not, under any circumstances, approach Belcher or Roidrage. Got it?" We salute him, like he's our general and we're about to go into battle. "Got it, Mini-E?"

"Aye aye, Captain," he says. I feel a pang of longing watching Elvis and his brother, seeing how they so clearly belong to each other. They fit. A matched set.

"Make a left," Elvis says. I turn, and immediately everything feels different. It's darker here—the Arthogus apparently used their tentacles to break most of the streetlamps. Guess they weren't fans of light bulbs! It also feels empty. There's a hollowness to the air, and it's almost too quiet. I get chills.

We see broken windows and broken glass. Couches with their guts spilling out in puffy white clouds. Houses with their front doors torn off.

"It's creepy," Zane says. We all jump when we hear a scurrying sound, almost like a snake's hiss. *Psssssssss.* Spike automatically goes fully pokey.

"Is this what you all do for fun?" Gertie asks. "Because . . ."

Zane quickly jumps in. "Not usually. I mean, we—" he stammers

"Because this is awesome," Gertie says.

"Who's there?" I call into the darkness when we

hear that weird noise again—*pssssssss*—but no one answers.

"Must be the wind," Elvis says.

I try to believe him.

Turns out the sound isn't the wind or a snake or a species of alien I have yet to meet that makes strange hissing sounds (which, honestly, seemed the most likely scenario).

"Come in, Number Five. I repeat, come in, Number Five," we hear, and immediately we can tell it's Officer Fartz's voice. Of course he'd be the one to make a *pssssssss* noise.

We didn't realize the walkie was set to an open channel. I doubt Elvis's dad, Michael, did either when he gave it to us.

"I'm here. And copy that, Number Five. Thank you for your help. But remember, all communications must be kept confidential," Lauren says, clearly having no idea that we can hear every word.

What must be kept confidential?

No doubt the right thing to do would be to turn

off the walkie. Zane looks at Gertie; Gertie looks at me; I look at Elvis; Elvis looks at Mini-Elvis, who looks back at Elvis; Elvis looks at me; I look back at Gertie; Gertie looks at Zane.

Zane blushes.

No one turns off the walkie.

"Roger that," Officer Fartz says.

"Who's Roger?" I ask, and Mini-Elvis giggles.

"It's what humans say when using devices like walkie-talkies: *'Roger that.' 'Copy that.' 'Ten-four, do you copy?'* You humans know so little about each other. It's wild," Mini-Elvis says.

We hear a few more *pssssssss* sounds and then Officer Fartz speaks again.

"I will not tell Michael. I repeat, I will not tell Michael," he says. Elvis shoots me a look: What could his mom and Officer Fartz be keeping from his dad? Is this why she's sending emails off base?

I shake my head. I have no idea.

"Copy that, over and out," Lauren says, and I think about her name in all caps on our wipe-it board.

It might just be that it's dark and we are in a spooky place, but I shudder.

CHAPTER EIGHTEEN

WHO MOWS FAKE GRASS?

A FEW MINUTES LATER, WE'VE DRIVEN DEEPER INTO THE Arthogus neighborhood, and we decide to park our golf cart on the side of the road. When we get out, Zane takes a flashlight from his pocket and turns it on, and we walk slowly behind its beam. This feels like the moment in a horror movie when you'd yell at the people on screen to turn around and run.

But we keep moving forward, step by step. Zane shines the light into a house on our right, and through the windows we can see a broken lamp and a turned-over couch. Something purple is splattered across the wall. I wonder if it's Arthogus guts.

"The Arthogus were obviously pretty angry when they left. They tried to destroy everything they could," Zane whispers.

"Including each other," Gertie adds.

"Where do you think Belcher and Roidrage are?" I ask. When I look away from the wall I feel the hair on my arms stand up. I notice something weird to the left of the road—it's a large field of fake grass that's been mowed into weird shapes.

"Why would you mow fake grass?" Zane asks.

"Looks like symbols, or maybe some Break Through language," Elvis says. "Though it's hard to see from this angle. We need to get higher."

We look around. Of course, there are no trees in sight.

"This is obviously some form of communication. Do you think . . . ?" I begin, but stop. "No. It can't be. Right?"

"Can't be what?" Elvis asks.

"You don't think that Roidrage and Belcher are using these designs to communicate with the Arthogus, do you?" I ask.

AAAACHOOO

CHAPTER NINETEEN

SPIDER-MAN TO THE RESCUE

ZANE—WHO IS THE BEST ARTIST AMONG US—COPIES THE symbols into a notebook so we can look them over more carefully later. We'll have to go to the library to see if they can be identified as Arthogusian or perhaps some other language. But first we need to complete today's mission: find Roidrage and Belcher.

"Why hasn't Area 51 cleaned up this neighborhood?" I ask in a whisper, which is my go-to voice when I feel creeped out.

"No one wants to come here. The Arthogus uprising was really traumatic. Occasionally, we'll have a school public service day where we clean up a house, but the neighborhood's pretty big. We only make a small dent each time," Zane says.

"And you'd be surprised by how many parents opt out their kids from participating. Both Break Throughs and humans. They feel like the houses in this neighborhood are bad luck," Gertie adds. "Like the Arthogus left it a mess as a warning."

"Yeah, I can feel the bad energy. It's activating my Spidey senses," Mini-Elvis says.

"You know about Spider-Man on Galzoria?" I ask.

"Who's Spider-Man? I mean it's literally activating my spider senses. Galzoria have sensory nerves on our legs and our pedipalps, just like spiders," Mini-Elvis says.

I'd define "pedipalps" for you, but I have no idea what it means.

"Well, you've all succeeded in creeping me out even more. So thanks for that," I say. I have goose bumps up and down my arms.

I think I hear Belcher.

NOPE, SORRY. THAT WAS ME!

A few moments later, we turn another corner, and this time we all spot Roidrage and Belcher at the same time. What we see is so strange and surprising, I gasp. The two of them are sitting on plastic beach chairs in the front yard of a freshly painted former Arthogus house. Their cheerful home even has nice new windows with fake flowers in the flower boxes.

"I bet Belcher's breath stinks," Zane murmurs.

"What are they doing?" Elvis asks. "This is weird."

"I think they're . . . knitting," I say, and almost burst out laughing. Of all the things I imagined them doing in their free time, knitting was not one of them.

THINGS SKY IMAGINED
ROIDRAGE AND BELCHER DOING:

1. Lifting weights

2. Torturing small animals for funsies

3. Giving each other tattoos

4. Making a plan for revenge

"They're knitting," Zane confirms.

"They're knitting sweaters," Elvis says.

"They're knitting sweaters for *each other*," Gertie says.

"They're knitting sweaters for *each other* while listening to a guided meditation," Zane says.

"Huh," I say.

"I'm a great knitter," Mini-Elvis says. "We learned it in preschool as a stress relief technique."

"Guess that's why they wanted yarn," Gertie says.

"Should we bother them?" Elvis asks, his voice sounding as nervous as mine. Somehow, it would have been less disturbing to have stumbled upon them bullying small children. This . . . is confusing and out of character.

What are they going to do next?

Break into song?

Smile?

Hug?

This obviously changes nothing. Belcher and Roidrage can knit and also coordinate the destruction of Area 51. I still put them on the top of my suspects list, despite the fact that Elvis's mom, Lauren, is obviously keeping some big secrets.

"You know what? Let's come back another day,"

I say, and when we all jump back into the golf cart, I don't even hesitate before breaking another rule. It feels like a matter of safety: I press the supersonic button and we race home.

CHAPTER TWENTY

OH MY,
PASTRAMI ON RYE

WHEN I GET HOME, STILL CONFUSED ABOUT FINDING ROIDRAGE
and Belcher meditatively knitting, I see my uncle
standing on the fake grass in front of our little pink
house staring up at the sky.

(There are no live plants in Area 51 because
all the oxygen they produce bothers the Break
Throughs, which is something I still haven't gotten used to. I can let Chill walk right through me,
no problem, but when I remember there isn't a
tree within sixty square miles, my stomach goes
queasy.)

What is Uncle Anish looking at? Is he wondering
whether the Killer Space Toilet is on track right now
to obliterate us at any moment? Is he thinking about
my mom and dad, like I often do while looking at
the sky? Is he making a wish?

"Hey," I say softly, not wanting to disturb the

silence. Unlike in the Arthogus neighborhood, the quiet here is peaceful. "You okay?"

"Of course," he says, turning to look at me. His tone is gruff, and if this had been six weeks ago, I probably would have felt a little bit hurt. But I've grown used to Uncle Anish, and I know that he's a softie underneath that tough exterior. When he was accidentally sent to Area 51 jail—a long story for another day (perhaps see *The Area Fifty-One Files,* book 1, #ad)—instead of worrying about whether he'd spend the rest of his life behind bars, all he worried about was me.

"When do you think it's going to happen? I mean, how much time do you think we have before they attack?" I ask. That seems to be one of the key missing pieces of information about this whole thing. I think about Mini-Elvis telling us that Break Throughs can have very different conceptions of time than humans.

"No idea. From the information I've gathered from Elvis's Galzorian parents—who, by the way, are lovely, but oh my, pastrami on rye, they are difficult to get a straight answer from—it seems likely that if we don't stop it, we'll be attacked within weeks." Uncle Anish says this to the sky, not to me—who is also Sky, but you know what I mean.

"It's strange to look up and realize there is someone—*someones*—out there who wants to hurt us," Uncle Anish says. "We've always been like a family here in Area 51, and we've always had a common purpose . . . with that one exception of the uprising." He mumbles this last bit, as if to downplay it.

"I still don't know much about what happened with the Arthogus," I say.

"Sky Patel-Baum, why haven't you read the Area 51 handbook?!" Uncle Anish gathers himself up until he is large and imposing, and I burst out laughing. He can't scare me into reading that gazillion-page book.

"Sorry, Uncle Anish," I say. "I'll get right on that."

"How's your UFO project coming along?" Uncle Anish asks.

"*UFO project?* Oh right, yes, my UFO project. It's going really well," I say, stuffing my hands into my pockets. I've always been a terrible liar. "UFOs are fascinating. I mean, there are so many different kinds and shapes and ways of entering the Earth's atmosphere. I could do research forever."

Spoiler alert: Sky does not get right on that.

Uncle Anish peers at me, suspicious.

"Hmph," he says, but before he can ask me any more questions, Mini-Elvis comes running across our fake lawn with Elvis chasing him, both of them giggling like maniacs. The Dino-parents follow them outside, smiling.

"Where is my camera? I need to take a picture of this," Dino-Mom says, and Dino-Dad smiles fondly at her.

"Around your neck, sweetie. Do you think the boys will get dirty playing? How often do you think they sanitize the grass?" he asks.

I'm mesmerized by the sight in front of me. I wish it didn't hurt to watch this: Elvis whooping joyfully while he tackles and then tickle-tortures his little brother. But I'd be lying if I said it didn't. My stomach knots, and a wave of loneliness passes through me.

Elvis is only a few feet away, yet he hasn't even noticed I'm here. In my short time on this earth, I've lost everyone I've ever cared about. First my parents, and then I was separated from my grandma. Is Elvis next? Will I lose him to his Galzorian family? Suddenly that thought feels a whole lot scarier than a killer space toilet.

CHAPTER TWENTY-ONE

NO ONE LIKES BEING ON HIGH ALERT

THIS MORNING UNCLE ANISH ISSUED A WARNING TO ALL of 51, which I think basically translates into "Get your bunkers ready" and "You'll likely have to go underground at a moment's notice." He didn't tell the residents why.

On the ride to school, we could see the news sinking in. Outside the commissary, humans and aliens lined up to stockpile supplies, and near the exit, everyone lined up again to barter with whatever they managed to get. No one seemed to be panicking. Yet.

Except, of course, those of us who know what the warning was about.

Luckily, Uncle Anish's bunker—which I had the pleasure of sleeping in last month when there was a false alarm and we thought more Zdstrammars had been kidnapped—is already fully stocked.

After the other day at Zane's, I really hope his mom or Agent Fartz replenishes their bunker. I think Mini-Elvis ate all the Mars bars.

I shouldn't be surprised that Ms. Moleratty corners me as soon as I enter the classroom now that we're on "high alert." Because Uncle Anish is head of the FBAI, she always assumes I have the inside scoop on Area 51 happenings.

It's also so very Area 51 that we still need to go to school every day despite the fact that an old Russian toilet may already be on its way to annihilate us. Also, did I mention it is summer and we still have to go to school?! IT IS SUMMER AND WE STILL HAVE TO GO TO SCHOOL!!! No one can accuse Area 51 of overreacting to threats or undervaluing education.

"What's going on, Sky?" Ms. Moleratty asks, and her tone makes clear she doesn't mean it as a hello. Everyone in Area 51 is on edge.

"Nothing much. I'm all ready for today's test on the Peeyous' digestive system," I say casually. "Man, they have a super-toxic soup in their bellies. Explains a lot."

Of course I'm not going to let on that I know anything. I promised Uncle Anish. Also, I really don't want to see what would happen if word got out.

"I mean, *what's going on?*" Ms. Moleratty says, waving her long ratlike nose in the air like it's a baton being raised to conduct an orchestra.

"I'm not sure what you mean, Ms. Moleratty. What's going on is: class is about to start," I say innocently. Does she really think I'll spill the beans? I may be new to Area 51, but I know this place is built on the premise of absolute secrecy.

"Okay," Ms. Moleratty says, her eyes narrowing suspiciously, and she plays with the charm on a chain around her neck that I've never

These lips are zipped.

These lips unzip for pizza!

noticed before. It says *BH* 💜 *LM* with a weird shape underneath it: a circle inside a circle. Why does it feel familiar? Where have I seen that symbol before? Does Ms. Moleratty have a partner?

The bell rings, and Ms. Moleratty claps her hands to get us to line up for vitals. Every day at Area 51 Middle School starts with her shooting at our foreheads with a weird laser and recording our vital signs in her notebook. Apparently, I'd understand the *why* behind this ritual if I read the Area 51 handbook. Guess I'll be kept in the dark on this one.

"Don't forget to bring in your permission slips for the Species Museum field trip tomorrow," Ms. Moleratty calls to the class as she zaps our foreheads. I've never been to the Species Museum, but Zane's mom works there and he says it's super cool.

"Sky! Yo, Sky!" Cubista, a Break Through who looks like a Picasso painting—all eyes and nose and mouth out of order—taps me on the shoulder with her foot, which happens to be attached to the back of her neck. She's always difficult to read, with her features all scattered like puzzle pieces, but even I can tell she's scared. "What's going on? I heard we're all going to die."

"We are not all going to die," I say.

"I overheard Elvis's mom talking to Agent Fartz the other day at the hardware store. She was like, 'I still haven't heard back, but yeah, maybe it doesn't matter because we're all going to die,'" Cubista says.

Lauren said that? Holy cannoli! The thought makes me feel itchy under my skin.

I glare at a Spotify named Shuffle who is sitting to my left. Normally, he turns down his volume during school hours—the Spotifies can't help picking up radio signals from all over the universe since their ears are basically radio satellites—but today he's blasting "It's the End of the World As We Know It." It is not helping with my nerves.

"Who's going to die?" a Splat asks. Their plasma is neatly contained now and no longer leaking all over the hallway.

"Chill, everyone," Chill says, and it's just the

thing to break the tension. The rest of the class bursts out laughing.

I suddenly remember Dino-Dad saying we have a 13.785 percent chance of survival. I shiver again, but this time it has nothing to do with Chill.

13.785 percent.

Those are some scary odds.

At lunch, Zane, Elvis, and I gather at our usual table in the back corner, and I smile when Gertie joins us. We need to work on our plan, and we can definitely use her giant brain. Today, we're eating spaghetti and eyeballs. No, that's not a typo. Our lunch ladies are Retinayas, who are prone to shedding their eyeballs. The good news? They're high in protein. Also, their eyeballs are satisfyingly crunchy. Kind of like potato chips.

"We need to figure out the big secret between Lauren and Fartz," I say. Elvis glowers at me. I don't think Elvis has ever glowered at me before, and the itchiness I felt earlier only gets worse. I feel like my whole world is unraveling in slow motion. I'm so anxious, I can't even squeeze out a Fartz pun.

I take a bite of my spaghetti, taste something that is neither eyeball nor noodle, and reflexively gag.

"Don't worry. That's just a blood vessel. Sometimes they detach from the cornea of the eyeballs," Gertie says.

"Gross," I say crankily.

"My mom says they're packed with vitamins," Zane says, and flexes his muscles. Yup, it's even creepier that a twelve-year-old is so ripped because he's been eating Retinaya body parts.

I push away my lunch. I prefer my Flintstones for my missing nutrients.

Suddenly, I feel something looking at me, and it's not the eyeballs on my plate. I glance up and see Dino-Mom and Dino-Dad with their tiny hands against the glass of the cafeteria's windows.

What are they doing here? Parents aren't supposed to be at school, I think resentfully. *This is my time with Elvis.* I know I'm not being fair, but I'm not sure I can help it.

"Your parents are over there," Gertie says, and nudges Elvis. Elvis looks at the window, and for a second, I see his face fall.

"Hi, darling," Dino-Mom calls through the window, and then looks down at the map in her hands. "We're just doing a little sightseeing. So this is your school, huh? It's very . . . pink."

"Did you sanitize before eating?" Dino-Dad

asks, and Elvis, after looking around the room to see if anyone is watching, gives them a peace sign.

"Are you going to finish that?" Zane asks me, barely noticing Elvis's parents. He reaches over to grab my plate before I even answer. "I love the stringy bits."

"Well, have a great day, my cutie-patootie-sweetie-muffin-lamb-chop," Dino-Mom says, and waves. This time, there's no doubt about it: Elvis winces.

"They are everywhere," he mutters under his breath. I want to ask him what he means. I'd love for my parents to be everywhere, and I mean that literally. Like I'd love for them to be here on Earth with me right now looking through the window and calling me ridiculously cute names—or anywhere else on Earth, for that matter. I'd be overjoyed.

I look closely at my best friend. He's tired and stressed and even crankier than I am. Normally, I'd grab his hand, but I feel a space open up between us, like it's a solid thing. Something almost impossible to cross.

So instead, I look away.

··· CHAPTER TWENTY-TWO ···

FIELD TRIP!

"WILL YOUR MOM BE GIVING OUR TOUR?" I ASK ZANE WHEN we arrive at the Species Museum for our field trip the next day. I've never met his mom, and I'm curious to see what she's like. I can't imagine anyone wanting to marry Agent Fartz. You can't have a name like that and not stink.

"Nah. She's been working around the clock to finish the new exhibit on the Spotifies, but she's off today. She said Ms. Spitz will be showing us around," Zane says.

The Species Museum, as its name indicates, is a museum dedicated to all Break Through species that the scientists at Area 51 have identified so far. The highlighter-yellow building is domed, and pictures of various aliens dancing together are painted into a beautiful mural on the ceiling. Each room off the main hall is dedicated to a different planet. Some of

them I've never even heard of: Choculus. Egglandia. Stinkerton.

I wonder if there's a museum in a distant galaxy dedicated to humans and planet Earth.

THE HUMAN MUSEUM

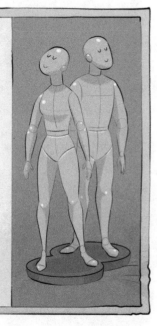

FAMILY NAME: Homo sapiens

DEFINING CHARACTERISTICS: They are their own worst enemies but are also capable of radiating pure love; both a complicated and simple species; also enjoy something called "sarcasm."

LIFE SPAN: on average 72.74 years

POPULATION ON X: 0 (humans, well behind the rest of the species in the universe, have yet to master space travel)

HOSTILE OR FRIENDLY: To Be Determined

Probably.

"I forgot to tell you my mom said we should all bring our raincoats," Zane says to us, but I don't get to ask why, because Ms. Spitz stands in front of our group and claps her hands three times to get our attention.

"One, two, three, eyes on me," she says, which has the unintended effect of having about eight

bajillion eyeballs turn to her, as there are quite a few Retinayas in the crowd.

Ms. Spitz is a tall woman with cropped pink hair and round cheeks that remind me of a chipmunk's. I wonder if she's related to Ms. Moleratty. Ms. Spitz is wearing a T-shirt with the words *SPACE FANATIC* on it, and her pants are decorated with planets. Even her belt matches the theme. It's patterned with astronauts in puffy white space suits.

After her introduction, Zane, Elvis, Gertie, and I quietly move from the front of the crowd to the back. It turns out Ms. Spitz sprays saliva when she talks, and we don't want to get showered. Better to leave the Mistyopolises in the front, since their skin is water repellant. In other words, they have natural raincoats. Come to think of it, I wonder how they shower.

"I'm here to talk to you about our museum but also about NEVER. EVER. GIVING. UP. ON. YOUR. DREAMS," Ms. Spitz says so emphatically that I hear her in all caps. She's borderline yelling at us. "I've always wanted to go to space, to experience the glory of zero gravity, to visit other planets, especially as we watch this one dying in real time."

"Well, that's uplifting," I mutter to Zane, who shushes me.

"I wasn't accepted into the space program, so I didn't become an astronaut, but I do have the privilege of working here. And who knows? Maybe one day I will get my chance to see firsthand what's out there," Ms. Spitz says. For a moment it looks like she might be crying. Or maybe that's spit on her face?

Either spit or regret. I'm not sure.

Nope, definitely tears. Wow.

"She's one of those," Elvis says under his breath.

"One of what?" I ask.

"You know, the type of people who find their

way to Area 51 not because of a special talent, but because they're obsessed with all things space," he says, rolling his eyes. He looks tired again today. I wonder if he's getting enough sleep in his crowded house. "So annoying."

"I think it's kinda cool that she's so passionate about something," I say. I wonder if I'll ever be that passionate about anything. The thing I'm most passionate about at the moment is not dying in a toilet explosion.

"Which room shall we start in?" Ms. Spitz asks, wiping away her tears with a handkerchief decorated with . . . wait for it . . . the NASA symbol. Various Break Throughs yell out their planets: Peeyou, Zdstrammaroos, Splatozia, Sanitizoria. "You know what? Let's make this fair. Let's start with a planet none of you have ever been to. Let's talk about the Arthogus!"

CHAPTER TWENTY-THREE

A TOUR OF THE SPECIES MUSEUM

WE FOLLOW MS. SPITZ DOWN A CORRIDOR AND INTO A darkened room, lit only by a projector showing videos on the wall. For the first time, I see on-screen what actual Arthogus look like, beyond Roidrage's creepy tattoo. They are bigger than I imagined, with two giant googly eyes centered on their forehead, and octopus-like tentacles that seem to curl in rage. In the video, they are patrolling the streets of the Arthogus neighborhood, scurrying along with their suckers.

Ms. Spitz stands at the front of the room and starts to narrate.

"As all of you know from your Area 51 handbook, the Arthogus uprising occurred on July 4, 2018, and both human and Arthogus lives were lost. It is the only time in Area 51 history when a Break Through species took up weapons against the

Dude, they're scary!

human population. Hopefully, it was also the last," Ms. Spitz says.

"A killer space toilet sure sounds like a weapon to me," Zane whispers.

"Do you remember the uprising?" I ask. Zane shakes his head.

"They kept most of the details from the youngest on base. They didn't want to scare us," Zane says.

I'm fascinated watching the Arthogus slither

their way past typical Area 51 houses, only stopping to flick their large tentacles at other Break Throughs and children who make the mistake of walking nearby. It looks like they enjoy making kids cry.

If I squint, though, I can see someone familiar walking with an Arthogus in the background. They look like they're chatting and laughing.

"Ms. Moleratty, is that you?" Gertie asks, shocked, and Ms. Moleratty nods.

"That was Big Head. He was the love of my life," she says sadly, touching her necklace.

I look again at the jewelry dangling from her neck. *BH* ♥ *LM*. *Big Head*. And that strange symbol—what is it? I still can't remember where I've seen those circles, and it's driving me bananas. I'll ask Zane later to check the symbols he drew in his notebook to see if there's a match.

Ms. Spitz continues with her presentation as if Ms. Moleratty hasn't said a word.

"From the moment the Arthogus arrived on planet Earth, there was tension. They expected to colonize Area 51 and claim it as a territory of the planet Arthogus. Area 51 resisted, and in the end, the Arthogus returned home, never to be heard from or seen again," Ms. Spitz says. Then she clicks a button and the screen changes.

"Is this why the Arthogus want to destroy 51? Because they're still angry about being sent back?" I ask Elvis in a whisper.

"I think they want revenge," Elvis says.

"But how would they be able to communicate with someone here in 51 if it's not through email?" I ask, because that's another piece of the puzzle I can't figure out. Not only do the Arthogus require ground control, but they need to be in constant communication with someone on base. Even though we know Lauren is keeping secrets, I can't believe she has anything to do with the Arthogus.

But if Ms. Moleratty was in love with an Arthogus . . .

Where is Big Head now, I wonder, and is it

possible she's still in touch with him? I look at my teacher, suspicion rising, and add her name to the list of suspects in my mind. (The wipe-it board will have to wait.)

Shuffle, the Spotify who had us humming BTS earlier, starts playing Bieber and the whole class groans, though for some reason it seems to perk Ms. Spitz up.

"Let's visit the planet Spotify next," she says, leading the way. Frequency Kenneth, another Spotify, changes his song to "Take Me Home, Country Roads."

☢ ☢ ☢

As we walk through the museum, I catch up with Ms. Moleratty. I need more information.

"What ever happened to Big Head?" I ask as gently as I can.

"He went back home." Ms. Moleratty's voice is scratchy and raw and tinged with sadness.

"That must have been hard for you," I say.

"Just so you know, he wasn't part of the uprising," she says. "He was against it from the start. But he couldn't stay. It would have been too hard to be the only Arthogus in Area 51, especially after everything that happened." Ms. Moleratty takes a tissue out of her pocket and blows her nose. I've never thought about what it would be like to lose someone to another planet. I wonder if Elvis has thought about returning to Galzoria. If I could lose him like that.

No. I shake the thought out of my head. I am not losing Elvis. I am just not.

"Big Head and I were going to get married," Ms. Moleratty continues.

"I'm sorry. Were you able to keep in touch?" I ask.

I squint at Ms. Moleratty, trying to decide if she looks shifty. She looks just like a rodent. In my opinion, all rodents look shifty.

CHAPTER TWENTY-FOUR

PEEYOU PUNK

"HOLY CANNOLI," I SAY, BECAUSE THE SPOTIFY ROOM IS A multisensory experience.

"It's amazing, right?" Zane says.

"I think this is my favorite room," Gertie says.

I take in the lights, the smell, the music, the 3D exhibit that breaks down exactly how the Spotifies pick up sound from all over the universe.

"Wait, does that mean they can hear us when we whisper?" I ask.

"I don't think so," Elvis says, and glances over his shoulder at Shuffle. "They pick up sonic waves and radio. It must be different."

"You know how you were curious about someone possibly sending emails to space?" Gertie asks us. "Well, this room got me thinking. Someone could *also* send messages via radio waves."

Hmm.

Gertie motions to a weirdly lifelike Spotify statue in the center of the room.

"I'm just saying those ears could be very, very useful," Gertie says.

Suddenly curious about something, I raise my hand.

"Ms. Spitz, I have a question about the Spotifies. Can they transmit radio waves as well as receive them?" I ask. Ms. Spitz smiles and looks at Shuffle and Frequency Kenneth.

"Would you like to take this one, kiddos?" she asks them.

"We can transmit, too," Shuffle says. "By the

way, want to hear some awesome punk music out of Peeyou? It's rockin'."

An hour later, we unexpectedly run into Elvis's parents in the Sanitizorian room. Dino-Dad looks like he's in heaven.

"This place is amazing. So clean!" he says.

"What are you doing here?" Elvis asks, the slightest edge to his voice.

"According to PlanetAdvisor, the Species Museum is number one on the Must See in Area 51 list!" Dino-Mom says, and puts on her glasses to read the map in her hand. "We also wanted to see the Great Pyramid of Giza, but apparently that's a little far from here."

"Oh," Elvis says. "Right."

"So many species, so little time," Dino-Mom says, and pats Elvis awkwardly on the arm.

"Well, we need to follow Ms. Spitz," Elvis says, smiling tightly. "But I guess . . . I'll see you later. At . . . home."

We leave them behind and continue next door to the Audiotooter room, which smells delicious. Zane, Gertie, Elvis, and I chat in the corner, surrounded by a cloud of rose perfume.

"Maybe the Spotifies are working with the Arthogus," I say.

"Just because someone is capable of talking with the Arthogus doesn't mean they're actually doing it," Zane says. He's friends with Frequency Kenneth, so I understand why he's getting defensive. He says he wants to put Ms. Moleratty at the top of our suspects list because of Big Head, but I think it's really because she gave us a B on our human spleen dissection project.

"Also, the Spotifies have no motive for destroying this place. They have a growing population. They seem happy here," Elvis says.

"I guess," I say.

"Though I do find it very annoying that the Spotifies play Christmas music before Thanksgiving!" Elvis exclaims. "I know the holiday season comes earlier to some planets, but that doesn't mean we should have to hear 'Jingle Bells' here in October."

I smile. It always makes me laugh when Elvis gets worked up over silly, small annoyances. His hair goes all messy, as if it wants to flee his cranky head.

He might be a little moody lately, but he is still and will always be my best friend.

"How about this?" Gertie proposes. "Let's put the Spotifies up on the wipe-it board suspects list, but below Belcher and Roidrage and Ms. Moleratty. And let's add radio waves as a possible way of communicating with the Arthogus."

"Deal," we all say, and though we've gathered a bit more information, I can't shake the feeling that we are no closer to figuring this all out.

CHAPTER TWENTY-FIVE

UNCLE ANISH HAS A DATE!

"I HAVE A MEETING TONIGHT," UNCLE ANISH SAYS, BUT HE isn't wearing his FBAI uniform. Come to think of it, this might be the first time I've seen him in regular clothes. He looks quite dapper.

"What sort of meeting?" I ask. "Because you look like you're dressed to go on a date." I don't add *in 1948*, because that would be hurtful. Also, I like the retro vibe the 51 thrift store—where everyone does their clothes shopping—gives the base.

Uncle Anish starts to cough, and then his coughs pick up so much steam that I have to hit him on the back.

"Sorry, just got something stuck in my throat," Uncle Anish says, flustered. "I'm not going on a date. I'm having dinner with OG2."

"Dinner? Ooh-la-la," I tease.

"Stop it. She's an astrobiologist, and I thought she might be able to help me with this whole Arthogus mess," Uncle Anish says, his face reddening.

This is interesting: Does my uncle have a crush? He's blushing the same way Zane does every time he looks at Gertie.

"Right," I say. "Sure."

"Sky Patel-Baum," Uncle Anish says in mock anger. "Are you teasing me?"

"A little," I admit.

"Then wish me luck," he says, and winks as he heads out into the night.

My uncle has given me strict instructions to eat dinner at Elvis's house, because he still doesn't fully trust me home alone. I'm not sure why, since in my six weeks at Area 51, I have not yet burned down his house or gotten into any real trouble, with the minor exception of that one time I got arrested . . . and the fact that I have broken a few laws. . . . Okay, fine, maybe I see where he's coming from.

When I get to Elvis's house, it's abuzz with activity. Everything feels more cramped with the new dino-sized visitors.

"Hello, Sky," Dino-Mom says, and pulls me into her small-handed hug.

"Hello, Sky," Lauren says right after that, pulling me into an even longer hug that feels slightly competitive with Dino-Mom's.

"Hello, Sky," Mini-Elvis says. "I'm not going to hug you."

"Hello, Sky," Elvis says. "I'm not going to hug you either, but I am going to take you to the backyard to get you out of this awkward family situation."

"Umm, what's happening?" I ask out of the corner of my mouth as I follow Elvis. We walk through the kitchen, where Dino-Dad and Michael are wearing matching ruffled floral aprons and making a lasagna.

"You know how my bio parents fell out of the sky last week?"

"Um, yeah," I say.

"And now they seem to be everywhere we go?"

"Um, yeah," I say.

"Well, my parents are pretending to be super happy that my bio parents are here. Which I know they are, but I *also* know they are secretly feeling very threatened. You should see them all tuck me into bed every night. It takes like two hours.

"Also this house is not meant for six people.

And Mini-E snores. So loud. I don't understand how someone so small can make so much noise. He sounds like a lion.

"I'm so tired, Sky," Elvis says. "And confused. About everything."

"I get that," I say, because I do. Sometimes even the really good stuff in life can feel overwhelming. My grandma and I used to have a word we used for when

that happened: *nervcited*. It means "nervous plus excited."

"Have you asked your mom about the email yet?" I ask. "Maybe it will help to officially cross her off our list."

"Not yet. I haven't had a second with her alone. But I will. I promise," Elvis says, though he looks worried. "Pinky promise."

"Seriously, don't worry about it. You have enough on your plate right now," I say.

"Who has enough on their plate?" Mini-Elvis asks, coming out to the backyard, his baby blanket trailing behind him. "Dinner hasn't even been served yet."

♣ ♣ ♣

Eating with Elvis's family is awkward. Lauren and Michael seem stiff and uncomfortable; they're constantly walking around the table refilling plates with lasagna, like the Earth revolving around the sun. Dino-Mom looks flustered; so far, she's lost her fork—which seems giant in her small hands—and dropped her napkin three times. Dino-Dad, on the other hand, has apparently invited a Sanitizorian named Squeak to dinner without warning Lauren and Michael so that Squeak can clean the table between bites. The problem is that Dino-Dad missed the part of the Species Museum tour where it noted that Sanitizorians eat five times more than the average alien species. I can see Lauren silently panicking that we'll run out of food.

Mini-Elvis plays on the ground with Spike and Pickles, oblivious to the strained atmosphere. I look at Elvis and give him an encouraging smile.

Just as Lauren and Michael are doling out Squeak's third serving, the Area 51 alarm bells start chiming. *Bong, bong, bong.*

"Oh no!" Lauren drops the spatula, which splashes sauce on the table. Squeak quickly goes to work cleaning. "That's the 'we're under attack' alarm!"

She ushers us all toward their hatch and grabs her walkie. After listening for a moment, she turns to us.

"Incoming space junk," she says. "Area 51 Middle! They think it's a test run for the big one!"

Elvis and I look at each other, and we have one of our beautiful friendship mind meld moments. Without saying a word, we both know that we're going to make a run for it.

With all the commotion from the parents—I hear Dino-Dad ask Michael, "When was the last time you dusted down here?" as he's led down the stairs into the bunker—we slip out the front door without any-one noticing. We head straight for Elvis's golf cart and hop in. Area 51 Middle is under attack, and we want to be there to defend it.

If any moment ever called for the supercharge button, it's this one—sorry, Uncle Anish!—so I press it and we zoom toward school.

"AHHHHH!" we scream when Mini-Elvis, Pickles, and Spike poke their heads up from the backseat and scare the Honey Nut Cheerios out of us.

"Did you think we'd miss this?" Mini-Elvis asks, grinning, as if this is all fun and games and not extremely serious business.

"Wipe that smile off your face, Mini-E," Elvis says, very stern and big brother–like. "This isn't a joke!"

"I know," Mini-Elvis says. "But I always dreamed of going on important missions with my big brother, and now here we are!"

"Aww, Mini-E," Elvis says, and reaches back to tousle his hair.

This would be an adorable moment—I'd maybe take a picture for Dino-Mom—if we weren't rush-ing toward an Arthogus attack. Test or not, it's still terrifying. I don't even have time to feel jealous.

I look up at the sky and see a big metal box head-ing right toward us. I look back at Elvis.

"We maybe should have thought this through," I say, wondering if this is the moment Elvis and I die because we were too stubborn to get in the bunker.

CHAPTER TWENTY-SIX

CLOUDY WITH A CHANCE OF FECES

"STOP BEING DRAMATIC," MINI-ELVIS SAYS, LOOKING UP at the space junk coming our way. "Its velocity will absolutely damage the building, but we are too far away to actually get hurt by any of the debris."

The word *debris* comes from the French, for "waste" or "rubbish."

"The building has been cleared," a manly voice shouts as we pull up near the middle school. I see Agent Fartz, looking official as he starts wrapping caution tape around the perimeter. "Everyone get in your hatches and keep your distance."

Before I can wonder where Uncle Anish is, I see him running up while holding OG2's hand. She's dressed for a date too, in a super-cool flapper dress that looks like it's from the 1920s. Sometimes people get lucky with their used-clothing rations. Last week, Zane wore a 1980s fluorescent tracksuit with built-in shoulder pads and patent-leather tap shoes. Apparently, he was less lucky at the Area 51 thrift store.

When Uncle Anish sees me, he drops OG2's hand—ha! I knew it was a date!—and glowers.

"Do you not hear the alarm?"

WHAT ARE YOU DOING HERE??

"We're here to help," I say, which is of course the exact wrong thing to say. I should have said, "We are on our way home, sir, and we will be in a bunker ASAP."

"How many times have I told you that you are not an FBAI agent? You are a TWELVE-YEAR-OLD GIRL!!!" Uncle Anish shouts.

"I'm not sure what my age and gender has to do with this," I say, but before Uncle Anish can respond, Agent Fartz is grabbing his elbow. Uncle Anish has bigger things to deal with right now than me being a terrible listener.

He turns to Fartz, furious. "Give me the stats!"

"Okay, it's one hundred miles away and has a diameter of eight feet. We still aren't sure what it is exactly, but it looks like a container holding something. Could be a biological weapon," Agent Fartz says, calm and in control. I forget that to become an FBAI agent you need to train for years. I bet they teach you how to be chill under pressure.

I shiver. I am not chill under pressure. Even Chill is not chill under pressure. I just saw him running through the crowd a minute ago screaming "Help!"

"We have to assume the worst and hope for the best," Uncle Anish says. "Is there anything we can do to stop it?"

He asks this question of no one in particular, and we all go quiet. We have numerous space experts here, including a world-renowned astrobiologist (OG2), not to mention a ton of Break Throughs who have actual space travel experience, and not a single one pipes up with a reasonable suggestion.

"Look, it says ISS on the side," Mini-Elvis says, pointing at the object in the sky that is falling with what is now alarming speed. "So it must be from the International Space Station. And wait: what are those words?"

I'll have pizza for my last meal, please!

We all squint up.

"It says . . . Feces Containment System," I say. "What's that mean?"

"Nooo! Nooo! Noooooooooo!" Uncle Anish screams, but it's too late. By then the containment system has hit the roof of Area 51 Middle School, splattering feces everywhere.

As it lands on me, I suddenly remember that *feces* is a fancy word for poop.

· · · CHAPTER TWENTY-SEVEN · · ·

CALL OF DOODY

"WHAT IS THIS STUFF?" MINI-ELVIS ASKS, WIPING HIS FINGER through the brown goo on his sweatshirt. I guess there are still some things he hasn't seen on his many trips through the universe.

"Put it this way: it's not chocolate," Elvis says, and not for the first time since I've been in 51, I am very envious of the fact that Galzoria have no sense of smell.

"It's poop!" I yell, gagging. "We are covered in astronaut poop!"

"Which is human poop," Elvis points out.

"This is endangered feces," Mini-Elvis says. "Get it? Like endangered species, but feces?"

OG2 winces, either at the terrible joke or the fact that her lovely flapper dress is ruined.

"At least it wasn't a biological weapon. Or at least, not a biological weapon in the traditional, toxic sense," OG2 says. I admire her ability to see the glass as half full. I am currently seeing the glass as half full too. *Half full of poop.* "But it would be dangerous to eat the stuff."

She says this looking at Mini-Elvis, who obviously knows better.

"Shouldn't it have frozen?" Uncle Anish asks, and I have to admit I'm impressed that he can actually think about scientific principles right now. All I can think about is . . . well, *poooooop.*

"I bet it warmed with the acceleration into the Earth's atmosphere. Either that or the Arthogus put a heating element in the unit. If you're going to attack with poop, you want it defrosted," OG2 says. "This was definitely a test run for their real attack. This was mostly soft materials. Poop in a box. An actual toilet will be way more deadly."

Uncle Anish nods like this makes total sense to him, though it doesn't make much sense to me. Unfortunately, Area 51 Middle School looks like it has taken a direct hit and is badly damaged. The roof is caved in on one side, and the windows are all broken. At least Agent Fartz's caution tape kept us all far enough away from the flying glass.

The building looks like it belongs in the Arthogus neighborhood now, though it smells way worse. My brain flashes for a moment on the symbol on Ms.

Moleratty's necklace, and I suddenly remember where I've seen it before: graffitied on the side of an Arthogus house.

I wonder what that means—if this clue bumps Ms. Moleratty higher on our suspects list—but I have more pressing concerns at the moment.

See, I have never been splattered head to toe with human poop before, so I'm not sure how I'm supposed to react. This is grosser than dissecting a human spleen. This is grosser than the time Elvis, Zane, and I got locked in the toilet at FBAI headquarters. This is grosser than the video my grandma once showed me about childbirth. This is grosser than when Spike gave me a dead rat for my birthday.

Insert grossest thing you can possibly imagine here:

_____

_____.

This is grosser than the grossest thing you could possibly insert here.

I need a shower this minute. No, I need to have already showered. No, I need to go back in time and take Uncle Anish's warning that "curiosity killed the cat" way more seriously. In this case, curiosity poured feces (dung, doo-doo, excrement, stool) on the girl, but that doesn't have as good a ring to it.

THIS SHOULD BE FUN!

Uncle Anish's golf cart is nearby, so I start to run toward it, already imaging how good it will feel to be clean again and not smell this horrific smell.

"We weren't just pelted with human feces, we were pelted with *old* human feces," I cry.

"Think of it as vintage," Mini-Elvis says. I could vomit.

"Don't even try it!" Uncle Anish yells. "You are not getting that shhhhh . . . tuff on my cart. You are walking home, young lady."

"Ugh," I say.

"Serves you right for not getting in the bunker." Uncle Anish says this with as much dignity as a person can muster when there is poop in his hair.

Insert your favorite word for poop here:

_____!

CHAPTER TWENTY-EIGHT

TAKE THE GIRL OUT
OF THE POOP

I AM FINALLY CLEAN. I TOOK A SUPER-LONG SHOWER, WHICH was in violation of Area 51 water rules, but Uncle Anish said that as head of the FBAI he was making a new rule that we could shower as long as we wanted in times of feces attacks. He also took a super-long shower, as I imagine every other human and Break Through who got splattered did.

Uncle Anish and I also went around the house spraying air freshener to cover up the terrible smell. Apparently, you can take the girl out of the poop, but you can't take the smell of poop out of the girl.

I wonder if I will ever be able to eat again. Oh man, if I do, the food will go through my digestive track, and then I'll have to . . . No, no, no. *No*. Never again. I will not think about it.

"So how was your date before it all went to feces?" I ask.

"It wasn't a date," Uncle Anish says, blushing again. "Did you know that the study of poop is called scatology? It's an actual area of scientific inquiry. You can do all sorts of things with human waste. Use it as fertilizer, for example."

"Are you really trying to distract me from your date with more talk about doo-doo? Now that it's all said and dung, I think this is getting a little ridiculous," I say. Even Uncle Anish giggles at that one.

"Fine. It was a sort of date, though I did also want to ask her about astrobiology stuff. Anyhow, I think I really like her," Uncle Anish says, then covers his face with his hands. "It's been a long time since I went out on anything even close to a date, so please don't tease me too much."

"I won't tease you at all. But for what it's worth, I really like OG2," I say.

"Right, because you met her when you were breaking and entering at Telescope Hill," Uncle Anish says disapprovingly.

"She told you that?" I ask.

"Yup."

"Well, maybe I don't like her that much after all," I say, and Uncle Anish smiles.

"Quick question," I ask. "Have you seen the weird symbols mowed into the fake grass near the Arthogus neighborhood?"

Things have been so hectic we haven't had a chance to go to the library to try to decipher what we saw the other day.

"What were you doing near the Arthogus neighborhood?" he asks.

"You know. UFO project research," I lie. Uncle Anish raises an eyebrow. Of course he knows better than to believe me.

"Those aren't weird symbols. Those are Peeyou wedding announcements," he says.

"What?"

"It's a tradition. When Peeyous get engaged, they like to permanently mark the occasion somewhere. They used to do it with smell. Now, because everyone complained about the stench, they draw symbols in cement instead, or sometimes they use tattoos.

Mowing fake grass seems to have become the new trend," he says.

"Right," I say. "So it's *not* a way to communicate with the Arthogus."

"Nope, sorry. Not even close, Nancy Drew," Uncle Anish says, and we laugh.

☢ ☢ ☢

We don't get to relax for long, though. Pretty soon, Uncle Anish is called back to FBAI headquarters on his walkie because Area 51 is in a state of panic. I look out the window and realize that whoever summoned Uncle Anish wasn't joking. It's alien mayhem out there.

Elvis, Mini-Elvis, Spike, and Pickles come over as soon as Uncle Anish leaves, and we call Gertie and Zane to join us. We gather in the bunker again, because *snacks*—and talk through all the intel we have.

Zane writes on the wipe-it board. Of course.

"My stepdad agrees with OG2," Zane announces. "He said that the FBAI thinks the fecal attack on the middle school was a trial run for the big one. That the Arthogus wanted to see how accurately they could coordinate with someone on the ground and hit a target before they used the killer space toilet, which will be much bigger and heavier and therefore way more dangerous." Zane writes *TEST RUN* on the board.

"And my mom's still convinced they're communicating with someone here on base, but she has no idea how or who," Gertie adds. "They have to be here to report all the factors that are constantly changing in real time—like wind conditions and the angle of the Earth's rotation—so when the Arthogus are ready for the big one, they know exactly where to aim."

Zane writes *THE BIG ONE* on the board.

"I'm not sure if this matters, but Ms. Moleratty wears a necklace that has an Arthogus symbol on it," I say, finally remembering to relay this information to my friends.

Zane writes MOLERATTY = SUSPICIOUS on the board.

"Also, the whole base is on high alert. My step-dad left so quickly on his golf cart this morning he left skid marks," Zane says.

"You're saying Agent Fartz left *skid marks*?" I repeat.

Zane writes FARTZ PUNS ARE ALWAYS FUNNY on the board.

"Okay, so here's what we need to still figure out," Elvis says. "Number one: Who is the traitor on base? And number two: How do we stop them from communicating with the Arthogus before it's too late?"

Zane writes WHO and HOW on the board.

"My mom says that the FBAI, the astronauts of astronaut row, OG2, and the entire 51 police department are working on a plan to build a rocket that can be launched when the toilet is en route to knock it off course," Gertie says. "Apparently, they have some kind of net that will capture the space junk."

"That is so cool," I say, forgetting for a moment that none of this is hypothetical. *A rocket* might be the only thing that can save Area 51. That is not *so cool* at all.

"Focus, Sky," Elvis says. "Let's leave the adults to the rocket and do what we do best: solve mysteries. We need to learn more about the Arthogus. So we all know what we need to do. . . ."

"No," Zane says.

"No," Gertie says.

"No," I say.

"No," Mini-Elvis says. "Even though I don't know what we are all saying no to."

"We have to," Elvis says. "The future of Area 51 depends on it."

"No," Zane says.

"No," Gertie says.

"No," I say.

"No," Mini-Elvis says. "Even though I *still* don't know what we are all saying no to."

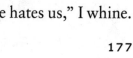

"Roidrage knows more about the Arthogus than anyone else in 51. He has an Arthogus tattoo. I heard he's even writing a book about them! We have to talk to him," Elvis says.

"But he hates us," I whine.

177

"They were *knitting*," Gertie says, like knitting is a bad word.

"We need to be brave. Area 51 Middle has been attacked! School is indefinitely canceled! We need to save this place!" Elvis says.

"School is indefinitely canceled?!" Zane, Gertie, and I all exclaim at the same time. "Woooohooooo!"

Zane writes SCHOOL IS CANCELED on the wipe-it board.

"Not for me," Mini-Elvis says sadly. "Area 51 Kindergarten is in a totally separate building."

"FOCUS!" Elvis yells. "LET'S GO SEE ROIDRAGE!"

Fine, but you have to sit on his tattooed side. I can't look at that thing.

Deal.

··· CHAPTER TWENTY-NINE ···

KNITTING INSTEAD OF PLOTTING

"DO YOU THINK ROIDRAGE AND BELCHER ARE STILL ANGRY at us for figuring out they kidnapped the Zdstrammars and getting them arrested?" I ask as we turn into the Arthogus neighborhood.

Zane looks at me like this might be the stupidest thing I've ever said.

Fair enough.

"Yeah, I think they still might be a little mad," he says sarcastically. " 'I love the people who sent me to jail,' *said no one ever.*"

"What's our game plan?" Gertie asks. I appreciate her levelheadedness. Zane, Elvis, and I have a tendency to jump into things without thinking them through first. Like right now, we are all crowded into a golf cart, about two minutes from coming face to face with the closest thing we have to a mortal enemy, and we haven't even discussed what we're going to say.

"Game plan? Let's just go and see what happens," Elvis says.

And maybe Gertie isn't so levelheaded after all, because she shrugs and says, "Sounds like a good game plan to me."

Belcher answers the door once Mini-Elvis rings, and I expect him to frown and yell at us to get off his lawn. But instead, shockingly, he smiles.

"Ooh, it's you! Please come on in. Officer Roidrage just took cookies out of the oven," Belcher says, and ushers us into a small but adorably decorated living room. The two of them made their banishment to the Arthogus community very cozy.

"We don't get many visitors, so we are extra happy to see you," Officer Roidrage says. It's like he's a totally different person from the one I first met. He's not mean or aggressive or even slightly scary, despite his Arthogus tattoo. Instead, he's gentle, and his cookies are outrageously delicious. I wonder what's in these things?

Who is this new Roidrage?

"Umm, thanks," I say. I'm tempted to apologize for everything that's happened between us, but then realize I shouldn't. They kidnapped Zdstrammars! They tried to frame Uncle Anish and steal his job!

"Listen, we're really glad you're here. We actually have something we need to say to you. We wanted to come to you directly, but we aren't allowed out of this neighborhood," Officer Belcher says. "So please let us take this opportunity to say how truly sorry we are for everything we did."

I blink. Did that just happen? Did Belcher actually apologize? To *us*?

"Yes. We apologize from the bottom of our hearts," Officer Roidrage says. "I've always been taught that when you do something wrong, you should offer a sincere apology and then ask what you can do to make it right. We obviously can't go back in time and not do what we did, but we are trying to make things right by cleaning up this neighborhood and dealing with our anger issues." Officer Roidrage takes a sip of tea.

"But if there is anything else we can do, please let us know," Officer Belcher says.

I look at Elvis and Zane, shocked. This is not what we expected.

"Thank you," I say. "And thank you for the apology."

"I'd like some cow's milk, please," Mini-Elvis says. "I hear that Earthlings like to dunk their cookies in it, and I'd like to experience that while I'm here."

"Umm, sure," Officer Belcher says. "Who are you, again?"

"I'm Mini-Elvis, from the planet Galzoria. It's a delight to make your acquaintance," Mini-Elvis says, and then curtsies. "Oh wait. You're not royalty. Not supposed to curtsy. Sorry, advanced human nonverbal communication isn't taught till first grade on Galzoria."

"We'd like to ask you some questions about the Arthogus," I say, turning to Roidrage. As promised, Elvis is sitting on his tattoo side, and from this angle, Roidrage looks relatively normal. Not like someone who would find it fun to chop up small children and then grill them like shish kebabs.

"Sure. By the way, are you Elvis?" Officer Roidrage turns to Elvis curiously. "You used to look just like the boy who bullied me in middle school. But now you look like Richard Simmons."

"Yes, I'm Elvis. Who is Richard Simmons?" Elvis asks.

"He was a famous aerobics instructor in the 1980s who had curly hair and a sweatband. He seemed like a genuinely kind dude. I used to exercise to his *Sweatin' to the Oldies* with my mother," Officer Roidrage says. "Huh. Must be all the yoga and meditating and gardening and coloring books and the anger support group. It's changed my perception of you."

"That's great," Elvis says, and I feel genuinely relieved. The way Officer Roidrage used to look at Elvis made me shiver.

"Ask me anything you want about the Arthogus," Officer Roidrage says. "I'm an open book."

☢ ☢ ☢

An hour later, I know more about the Arthogus than I ever thought possible, but we're no closer to figuring out who the traitor is on base.

"Honestly, there are a million ways to communicate with them. They are a highly evolved and communicative species. I don't think the question is *how* someone is talking to them. It's more *why* someone would be talking to them," Officer Roidrage says. I imagine Zane writing this down on the wipe-it board in his mind.

"Interesting," Mini-Elvis says.

"Do you know why I got this tattoo?" Officer Roidrage asks, and we all shake our heads. "Because every time I look in the mirror I want to remember the uprising and my commitment to 51."

"Huh," I say, surprised. I figured he got the tattoo to be as scary as humanly possible to the Break Throughs and, well, everyone else.

"And yes, for a minute there, my own ambition got the best of me, but what matters is how much I love this place. Anyone who does would never, ever intentionally communicate with the Arthogus," Officer Roidrage says. "They'd have to love something else more."

These words linger in my brain. *They'd have to love something else more.* My mind flicks to Ms. Moleratty and Big Head.

BH ♥ LM.

Could she love Big Head more than 51?

"So just to be clear, neither of you is plotting to destroy the base?" Gertie asks straight out, without even a little bit of fear. Maybe it's the brightly speckled cookies and Belcher's bunny slippers, but these two are decidedly less scary today.

"Nope. We've been too busy knitting to plot anything like that," Officer Roidrage says.

"I believe them," Zane whispers to me, and I have to admit, I believe them too. Which on one hand is fantastic: I really like the new Roidrage and Belcher, and I very much want to take them up on their invitation to come back for more homemade cookies. On the other hand: there will be no cookies to eat (or Roidrage and Belcher, or us) if we don't figure out how to stop the killer space toilet.

· · · CHAPTER THIRTY · · ·

MY ENEMY IS
NOW MY FRIEND

WHEN WE GET BACK FROM OUR LOVELY AFTERNOON WITH
our former enemies Belcher and Roidrage, we drop
off Gertie and Zane at their houses. Then Elvis,
Mini-Elvis, Pickles, Spike, and I come home to find
Elvis's parents—both sets of them—waiting for him
on the front lawn.

"Is everything okay?" I ask, hopping out of the
cart. I feel nervous. The last time Lauren and Michael
waited out on the lawn like this it was to tell me that
Uncle Anish had been arrested. They have the same
crease between their eyebrows again. Whatever this
is, it isn't good news.

"Umm, not really," Lauren says in a strangled
voice. Michael puts a hand on her shoulder.

"It's going to be all right," Michael says soothingly.

"What's going on?" Elvis asks. "You're freaking
me out."

"Well, there seems to have been a misunderstanding," Dino-Mom says, stepping closer to Elvis.

"A misunderstanding?" Elvis asks in a quiet, scared voice.

"I recently sent an email with the help of Agent Fartz to a contact in Washington, DC, to get housing for your . . . for them," Lauren says, pointing at Dino-Mom and Dino-Dad. "I was hoping they could take the house next door so you could keep living with us but you could still see them all the time. I didn't want to tell anyone and get your hopes up before I had an answer."

Hope the misunderstanding involves the accidental delivery of an XL pizza!

"And Washington said no," Elvis says, his voice flat and sad.

Well, this explains her email off base and the walkie-talkie conversation. I strike her from the suspects list in my mind, though to be honest, I never really believed there was any way Lauren could want to hurt us. There's nothing she loves more than Area 51, except Elvis.

"Actually, they said yes," Lauren says. "But that's not the problem."

"Then what's the problem?" Elvis asks. I put my

188

hand in his. Whatever he's about to hear is obviously going to be very, very bad. He was there for me when Uncle Anish got sent to jail. I'll be here for him, whatever this is.

"The problem is that we are not staying," Dino-Mom says.

"You're not?" Elvis asks.

"*We're* not. You're coming back to Galzoria with us!" Dino-Mom says, again with her mini jazz hands.

"I thought you knew we'd be going back," Dino-Dad says a little later, when we are all slightly less hysterical. We are in the backyard, eating a Code 61159 (half sausage, half eggplant). Spike seems to be the only happy one here. "We were sent here by the Galzorian president to warn you all about the space junk and then head right on back home after we had a vacation."

"But when I said we need to look for more permanent accommodation, you said 'Sure, sure,'" Lauren says. Her cheeks and ears are flaming pink. I can't tell if she's devastated or furious—maybe both.

I feel the same way.

"I meant sure, we'll stay with you for now," Dino-Dad says. "But obviously we can't stay here permanently. The germs alone are reason to leave."

"I like it in 51," Mini-Elvis says. "We don't have pizza on Galzoria. Or Earthling friends."

"But what if . . . what if I don't want to go back?" Elvis asks nervously. Pickles has settled into his lap and uses his tail to gently pat Elvis on the chest.

"Darling, of course you're coming back to Galzoria with us. It's your home," Dino-Mom says.

"But *this* is my home," Elvis says. He doesn't signal at the house behind us; instead, he's looking at Lauren, Michael, and me. As if *we* are his home. My heart grows in my chest. That's what friendship is, after all.

I'm not sure how I can survive here without Elvis, when *he* is the biggest reason I think of this place as home.

What would Area 51 be without him?

"Earth can't be home, Elvis," Dino-Mom says, and though she doesn't say, *Duh, everyone knows that,* we can all hear it anyway.

"Yes it can," Elvis says.

"We learned in preschool that the English word *home* can also be used to mean the place you feel like you most belong," Mini-Elvis says. "And as you grow roots in new places—not actual roots like a tree, but emotional connections—your home can change."

"Maybe for me that's here," Elvis says, tears shimmering in his eyes.

"Maybe for me too," Mini-Elvis whispers. His words come out so quiet, I'm not sure I've heard him correctly.

"We are done talking about this," Dino-Mom says with a growl so loud and reverberating it sounds like it came from a real dinosaur. A dinosaur who has spotted a terrifying ladybug. "Now, has anyone seen my glasses?"

CHAPTER THIRTY-ONE

TEAM #SAVE51

AS ELVIS REACHES OUT AND HUGS LAUREN IN WHAT SEEMS to be a desperate clutch, Uncle Anish comes bursting out the door. (Because there is *never* a moment in Area 51 to let things sink in!)

"It's HUGE. Like giant. Like we are all going to die big-time," he says. He's so flustered and scared that I almost don't recognize him. The Uncle Anish I know is so stiff and calm and in control that sometimes he feels more robot than human.

Seeing him like this scares the beef jerky out of me.

"The space junk?" Lauren asks, kissing Elvis on the head while simultaneously whipping her walkie off her belt.

"Yes. Since it's shifted closer, OG2 was able to make new calculations using the instruments at Telescope Hill. It's big enough to destroy not only Area 51 but the entire state of Nevada," Uncle Anish says. He's breathless and sweaty and it's clear he ran here from wherever he was when he learned this information.

"Well, that settles it. Vacation over. We're going back to Galzoria immediately," Dino-Mom says. "You are all welcome to join us, though I'm not sure you humans will survive the transition to our atmosphere without special equipment. Now, where is my fanny pack?"

"No, not to Galzoria," Uncle Anish says. "But you need to leave Nevada. Lauren, Michael, you take the kids. I don't trust the bunkers. They aren't built for an attack of this size."

"You want us to run away?" Lauren asks, horrified. "You want us to break the most important rule of Area 51?"

"I want you to keep those who are most important to us safe. That's what matters. And in this case, that means getting Sky and Elvis out of here," Uncle Anish says. "Please. I promised to take care of Sky. I can't let her get hurt."

"I'm not going to get hurt," I say, but Uncle Anish isn't listening. There are tears in his eyes. His hands are trembling. His knees keep knocking together.

"Go pack up," Uncle Anish says. "I wish we could evacuate everyone on base and then the entire state, but we're not getting the go-ahead from Washington."

"Stop!" Elvis yells, and we are all so shocked Elvis is yelling that we freeze. "No one is going anywhere right now. Not even you."

Elvis points at his dino-parents.

"This base is full of some of the most wonderful humans and Break Throughs in the universe. Presumably there must be some decent people in Nevada as well," Elvis says.

"So?" Dino-Dad asks.

"So we can't run. We have to save them!" Elvis says.

How,
exactly?

CHAPTER THIRTY-TWO

CLEANUP ON AISLE 51

WE ALL DECIDE TO SLEEP ON IT, SINCE OGZ, USING SOME complex mathematical formula I do not understand involving size and velocity, has determined that we have at least a few days before we're obliterated. The toilet has already been launched, though its trajectory will change depending on the coordinates given by ground control—whoever that is.

Elvis and I have agreed to be optimists. A few days is more than enough time to figure out who is communicating with the Arthogus and reverse the space junk's course, right?

"My uncle said that if they can shift the junk's trajectory even a few degrees with the rocket, it will miss Earth entirely and either get caught in their giant net thingamabob or just hurtle off into space," I say to Zane, Elvis, and Gertie the next day.

"But my mom says they aren't sure of the coordinates. Finding our traitor will make their rocket net launch way more precise and increase the likelihood of success. To put it in hacking terms, we need to go on a phishing operation," Gertie says.

"Fishing?" Elvis asks.

"Phishing. With a *p-h*. Never mind. The point is they'll be able to reverse engineer the toilet's location if we get the info from ground control."

"So in other words, we need to figure this out," Zane says. "Our lives literally depend on it."

We are at the mandatory community cleanup of Area 51 Middle. It smells so disgusting that even with our noses and mouths covered with bandanas, it's hard not to gag. The cleanup is slow and tedious and stinky work.

The problem is that a lot of Area 51 residents did not show up to help. Apparently, everyone is in full panic mode. The news of the test attack spread faster than a delivery of a Code 61154, and Uncle Anish has called an emergency meeting for later today. The air feels supercharged with fear.

Ms. Spitz, our Species Museum tour guide, is walking around with giant black garbage bags labeled *To Keep!* She clearly lives by the reduce, reuse, recycle principle, because she keeps picking up and saving random objects that I can't imagine anyone having a use for even if they weren't covered in poop—a broken whiteboard, a broken windowpane, a broken solar panel. The theme here is that everything is broken.

"What are you going to do with all that stuff?" I ask her, wondering how she intends to get rid of the bad odor. Maybe she hired some Audiotooters to fart some rose scent on them.

"Oh, hi. Didn't see you there," Ms. Spitz says, and I take a step backward. I forgot about how a conversation with her can feel like a shower. "I'm in charge of the Fourth of July celebration, which is only three days away. Figured I could find a use for these things there."

"It's interesting that we have a July Fourth celebration here," I say. *Also interesting that July 4 is the anniversary of the Arthogus uprising,* I think. *Surely that can't be a coincidence.*

"Of course we do. Just because the rest of the United States doesn't know about us doesn't mean we don't still feel an attachment to our country. I am very patriotic," she says. "In fact, when I took my test to get into our space program, I wore red, white, and blue for good luck. Though I guess it didn't help enough."

Her face falls, and I feel a little bit bad for her. I don't yet have some big life goal, but I imagine it was sad for her to get to a point where she knows that no matter how hard she tries, she'll never get to space.

Because I don't want to talk about her dashed dreams anymore, I start to babble.

"Tell me more about the Fourth of July here! That sounds like fun!" I say overenthusiastically, remembering how my grandma and I used to sit on a blanket on the beach to watch fireworks back in California. My grandma's favorites were the red ones that opened like umbrellas in the sky and then fell like raindrops.

I shake away the memory. It hurts to think about the people I've lost. I wonder if next year, Elvis will be back on Galzoria, and my memories of him will hurt too. We haven't had enough time together yet for me to learn his favorite fireworks.

"Oh, it's a blast! Pun intended," Ms. Spitz says, and giggles. I can't help wondering if she didn't get accepted into the space program because of her over-active salivary glands. She'd fill her helmet with spit. "We have the species flying parade. It's the only day of the year we can get away with it, because if any-one far away notices anything strange in the sky, they'll just think it's fireworks."

"What about here on 51? Won't everyone be nervous about things flying in the sky, considering what's happening?" I ask, looking around. I take in the full scope of the damage to the school. The general mayhem. The sinking realization in my stomach that maybe we won't make it out of here alive.

Even worse, if we somehow magically do, Elvis will be on the next spaceship out of Area 51. I try to feel glad for him. Maybe he'll be happy to be in a place where others can see him in all his eight-dimensional glory.

No. That can't be right. *I* see him clearly. I know my best friend. I understand Elvis through and through, even if I can't see him in eight dimensions. He wants to stay here. With us.

"Well, apparently, *your uncle* agrees with you," Ms. Spitz says. She spits out the words *your uncle* like they taste bad. I'd hate to know what would happen if someone gave her bag of sunflower seeds; it would be pure hail. "At the all-base meeting this afternoon, we're going to vote about whether we should still hold the Fourth celebration. But I've put in so much work. We can't cancel it now. We *can't*."

"I can understand being disappointed," I say diplomatically, taking another step back from Ms. Spitz. Man, her saliva has incredible velocity.

"Disappointed is an understatement. I'll be devastated. If the base is going down anyway, don't we deserve a last hurrah?"

The *Titanic*

I guess that's one way to go.

CHAPTER THIRTY-THREE

GOING DOWN DANCING

"FIRST THE BAD NEWS," OFFICER GLAMCOP SAYS, AND RAISES her hand to quiet the crowd. Miraculously, it works. All eighty gazillion eyeballs are on her. "Yes, there is a large piece of space junk that has been launched and is currently being controlled by the Arthogus, and yes, they have a plan to aim it right at us within the next seventy-two hours or so. And yes, it's a toilet from an old Russian spaceship. And finally, yes, if it does hit us, it will annihilate not only Area 51 but all of Nevada."

"What's the good news?" a Sanitizorian yells from the crowd.

"Well, the good news is it hasn't hit us yet," Officer Glamcop says. The crowd erupts in boos, and I can't say I blame them. That doesn't really feel like good news.

"Hear us out." Uncle Anish steps up to the mic. "That means we have the next two days to figure out who on base is working with them, and if we can identify that individual, we can stop this thing from happening. If the Arthogus don't have exact coordinates, they can't aim the lavatory toward us.

"We're also working on a rocket net . . . ," Uncle Anish continues, but he's drowned out by the crowd.

"Rocket net?! Are they kidding?" a Zdstrammar squeals.

"That's exactly the attitude we need! Thank you for those questions. To begin with, if you see anything suspicious, let us know. Now, that doesn't mean you should turn on your neighbors. We are first and foremost a community, and we are not going to let that happen. But please be aware: we've set up a private line on our walkies for anonymous tips."

The crowd erupts again, though this time it's to shout complaints about other resident species. I hear one person scream, "The Peeyous are not using their air freshener allotment!"

"Thank goodness for the Audiotooters," another Break Through responds.

Another yells, "Make the Retinayas pick up their eyeballs! No one wants to step on them. The stringy bits get stuck to my flip-flops!"

"To be clear, the walkie is for tips about the space junk! Not about things that annoy you," Officer Glamcop says. The crowd goes silent.

"Now for the July Fourth vote. If you want to cancel the celebration, raise your hand," Uncle Anish says. Officer Betty White climbs onstage and starts counting votes.

What if you don't have a hand?

"Sorry. I should clarify. If you don't have a hand, raise any appendage," Uncle Anish says.

Uncle Anish holds the bridge of his nose, which I've come to learn is what he does when he's frustrated.

"Please just count somehow," he mutters to Officer White.

An hour and a half later, and after much counting and recounting—apparently, there was an issue with whether the Spotifies' antennae count as appendages—the votes are finally in.

"It's official. The party will go on! See you all here for the Fourth!" Officer Glamcop says.

"If we're going to be blown to smithereens, might as well go down dancing," Chill says next to me, which may be the most chill thing he's ever said.

CHAPTER THIRTY-FOUR

ALL IN THIS TOGETHER

AFTER FORTY-EIGHT OF OUR REMAINING SEVENTY-TWO HOURS, we still have not found the culprit. Uncle Anish puts in long days at the FBAI, and at night, he continues to beg Lauren and Michael to take me and Elvis and make a run for it. Of course, we all refuse.

Elvis, Mini-Elvis, Zane, Gertie, and I spend hours in Uncle Anish's bunker in front of the wipe-it board, hoping to have some sort of aha moment.

Instead, we end up eating a whole lot of space-themed candy bars and Code 61154s.

The truth is, though I should be focused on saving Area 51, I spend a lot of time already missing Elvis, even though he is usually right next to me. You would think by now I'd have gotten used to people (or I guess in this case, an alien) leaving me behind. But I haven't. I can't imagine waking up the day after Elvis leaves and taking the golf cart to school without him. I can't imagine not being able to walk next door when I want to see him.

I can't imagine Elvis not being my best friend.

✿ ✿ ✿

It's finally July 4, and we head to Telescope Hill for the spaceship parade and celebration and, you know, possible annihilation. The hilltop is littered with tarps of varying sizes that Ms. Spitz has laid out for everyone to sit on. Even though there's a sense of impending doom, there's also a feeling of camaraderie. We're all in this together.

Elvis and I share a single tarp, and I look over at my best friend.

"Stop worrying," he says.

"I'm not!" I say. "I think we'll figure out how to stop the space junk."

"No, stop worrying about me going back to

Galzoria tomorrow. No matter what happens, whether I'm here or there"—Elvis stops and points to the sky—"you'll always be my best friend."

Elvis squeezes my hand. He has promised repeatedly that Galzoria don't have mind reading capabilities, but I'm not so sure. Sometimes it feels like Elvis can read me like a book.

Ms. Spitz stands in the center of the four telescopes, which are roped off tonight, and she's wearing the strangest outfit I've ever seen. She has the windowpanes from Area 51 Middle as shoulder pads, puffed-out pants that look like they're stuffed with wall insulation, and a shirt that's made from welded metal. She must have gotten really unlucky at the thrift store.

"Ms. Spitz has always been a little strange," Agent Fartz whispers to us. "Do you think she's confused July Fourth with Halloween?"

"Her outfit looks like a bizarre makeshift version of the space suit I wore on my first trip to the moon," says Nell Legswole, Gertie's mom, as Ms. Spitz holds up her hands to quiet us.

"Humans and Break Throughs, welcome to the Area 51 Fourth of July celebration!" she says dramatically, and the crowd cheers. "Please make yourselves comfortable on your assigned tarps, and let's get this party started!"

"Sky?" Mini-Elvis tugs on my sleeve to get my attention. I realize with a pang that I'll miss Mini-Elvis and his outrageously large vocabulary and his ratty baby blanket almost as much as I'll miss Elvis. He's started to feel like my little brother too.

I put my arm around his shoulder and give a little squeeze.

"Yeah?" I answer. I don't look at him, because I'm mesmerized by the show. I saw the Galzorian landing, and of course I've seen many spaceships in the Species Museum, but I've never seen anything like this. Saucers and funnels and lights swirl above us in a moving mosaic. I wish everyone in the world could see a space parade. It would change the way they think about UFOs—not as something scary but as something beautiful.

"Show-offs," I hear Dino-Mom mumble under her breath.

"Didn't Nell say that whoever was working with the Arthogus would need special equipment to survive the attack?" Mini-Elvis asks.

"Yup," I say, half listening. Dino-Mom might be right—the Break Throughs are definitely showing off—but I don't care. I'm in awe. An alien species I don't recognize is currently painting fluorescent pictures above us, like 3D skywriting.

"Look." Mini-Elvis points toward Ms. Spitz, and I drag my eyes away from the show to look at her again. For the first time, I notice she has golf cart tires attached to her butt. I squint, remembering her picking up each of these pieces at the Area 51 Middle School cleanup. She must've had to wash off all the feces in order to put this together. She wouldn't have done that unless she had a very good reason.

I motion Elvis, Zane, and Gertie over and share Mini-Elvis's observation.

"That looks like protective equipment, doesn't it? Like how football players wear pads?" I ask.

"What's a football player?" Elvis asks.

"Never mind," I say, because I don't have time to explain football, which is a ridiculously complicated sport, even for those of us who've watched since birth. "But that stuff could help her survive an explosion!"

"Maybe," Elvis says.

"But what's her motive?" Zane asks. "Why would Ms. Spitz, who has worked at the Species Museum for fifteen years, want to destroy Area 51?"

I close my eyes, because I can't think with all the commotion around me. The sky parade is too distracting.

"Maybe her motive has nothing to do with Area 51," I say.

"What do you mean?" Gertie asks.

"Well, on the field trip, didn't Ms. Spitz make a huge deal about how she always wanted to go to space? This could be her way of getting there! Maybe the Arthogus plan to pick her up after the blast," I say, and as the words come out, they somehow feel true. I remember her lecture about never giving up on your dreams. I remember Belcher saying that someone would have to love something more than Area 51 to help the Arthogus. Perhaps Area 51 and the whole state of Nevada is the price Spitz is willing to pay.

Perhaps she loves the idea of seeing space more than she loves humanity.

"Listen, I'm obviously for bold fashion choices," Gertie says, "but that doesn't feel like fashion to me. That feels like function."

"If she's our culprit, how is she communicating with the Arthogus? We can't just accuse her without evidence," Elvis says. We all look back at Ms. Spitz, who stands in the center of the four telescopes in her handmade space suit, talking to the crowd.

If she *is* communicating with the Arthogus and passing along coordinates, I have no idea how she could be doing it.

CHAPTER THIRTY-FIVE

CONNECT THE DOTS.
LITERALLY.

WE REMAIN QUIET, WATCHING THE SHOW FROM OUR TARPS while we think. The air is cold up here, and the wind whips our faces. I'm wearing a hooded sweatshirt with no coat, and I have goose bumps.

"You're freezing," Elvis says, looking at my wrists. "Or very, very nervous. Raised hair follicles can be a sign of either."

"Yeah, I'm both, but mostly cold," I say. I pull my hood up, and then I lie down so I can watch the stars. I don't know my constellations, but the night sky feels organized, like there's a pattern I can't quite make out. I want to take my finger and draw lines connecting the stars, see if they make a picture. Once Elvis leaves, I wonder if I'll feel like I can see him when I look up. Will he feel like he can see me when he looks at the Galzorian sky?

No, I can't think about that now. I need to concentrate.

I *need* to figure this out.

Suddenly, I shiver. I sit up, then jump to my feet. I look around at all my friends and neighbors spread out on tarps around me.

"I think I figured it out!" I say.

"What? Where? How?" Zane asks.

"What he said," Gertie agrees.

"She's using a QR code," I say. "Look!"

"I have no idea what she's talking about," Elvis

says to Zane, shrugging. "Do you? What's a QR code?"

"No clue," Zane says.

Right. In some ways, Area 51 is far ahead of the rest of the world. And in many ways, it is far behind. We don't have cell phones or cable television here, or, apparently, football. There is no reason for those who were born on base to ever have seen a QR code.

A QR code is a series of squares . . . like this!

But I wasn't born on base. I was born in California.

"It's basically a pattern that when scanned can lead to an Internet site. I think *we're* the QR code!" I exclaim, apparently loud enough that Uncle Anish hears me.

"Hmmm," he says, blinking a few times as he digests this theory. Uncle Anish is tall, perhaps one of the tallest people I've ever met, so when he looks out at Telescope Hill, he has a higher vantage point than most of us.

"You mean the tarps," Uncle Anish continues.

Telescopes Hill

"Yes. I think they're

deliberately arranged so that they can be scanned from space as a QR code, which will give exact coordinates and information to the Arthogus!" I say.

SKY'S THEORY

"And Ms. Spitz organized this? Even the tarps?" Uncle Anish asks.

"Yes," OG2 says. "I was on patrol all week and saw her out here multiple times. She even drew lines where each piece should go. She had a whole complicated map that she kept redrawing. I assumed she was just trying to maximize the space. And she kept shifting things. Even at the last minute. Now I think she was acting as ground control, measuring wind speeds, gravitational forces, that sort of thing."

"And don't forget she's wearing a makeshift astronaut's suit," Gertie chimes in.

"Holy cannoli," I say.

"Oh my snoogles," Elvis says.

"You figured it out," Nell Legswole says.

"We need to arrest her," Agent Fartz says, on his feet, already pulling handcuffs from his back pocket. I wonder what else he keeps in there. "We can't let her rip."

There is no time for Fartz puns!

THERE'S ALWAYS TIME TO LET OUT A FARTZ PUN!

"Wait! First, we need to shift the tarps so the Arthogus can't scan the code and read the coordinates. We also need to use her measurements to launch our rocket net!" Uncle Anish points up at the stars. "Let's move before it's too late!"

We start with our own tarps, crumpling them up into balls and yelling to our neighbors to do the same. Uncle Anish spreads the message through his walkie-talkie, and soon the celebration turns frantic. Everyone is on their feet— well, at least those who have feet are on them—and tarps are being pulled up and thrown into a large pile.

"WHAT ARE YOU ALL DOING?!" Ms. Spitz yells. She's so angry that she's projecting saliva everywhere. She looks like a water fountain.

We don't listen, and within minutes Telescope Hill is a mess.

"NOOOOOOOOOO!!!" Ms. Spitz cries, dropping to her knees. "THIS WAS MY ONLY CHANCE!"

"You were going to destroy everything we've built here to help the Arthogus? Seriously?" I ask her.

But she doesn't answer me, because Agent Fartz is here now with Officer Betty White, cuffs out.

Fartz hands me a piece of paper with numbers scrawled on it, and I shout them to OG2, who, with the help of Nell Legswole, is currently setting up a large rocket. Apparently, it was brought up the hill in sections and reassembled at the top. When put together, it's impressive—the sort of rocket you'd see in a NASA launch on television. And yet I don't like looking at it. We've done our part. Now we have no choice but to hope this machine does its part.

I'd much rather rely on people (or Break Throughs) to save us than technology.

OG2 takes out a handheld device and types co-ordinates into it, reverse engineering the best course for the rocket.

"Count us down!" Nell Legswole yells to us. I cross my fingers and toes. Close my eyes and then open them again. Take a breath. This is it.

Please let this work.

"THREE, TWO, ONE," Elvis, Zane, Gertie, Mini-Elvis, and I yell in unison.

"And go!" OG2 says, and presses a button on her screen.

We all tilt our heads back and watch the rocket launch, which is almost, but not quite, as beautiful as the space parade.

A whoop goes up from the crowd. We did it! We really did it!

"What's that net made out of?" I ask Uncle Anish.

"Human hair," he says. "You know, reduce, reuse, recycle."

"Right," I say, like this isn't officially the grossest

thing I've ever heard—and I've been attacked by a fecal containment unit *and* have dissected a human spleen.

"Phew, I'm so glad Area 51 wasn't destroyed. What a great way to end our vacation," Dino-Mom says.

"When we went to Peeyou, all we did was lounge on the beach. This was much more exciting," Dino-Dad says.

"Well, we're so grateful you warned us. Thank you both from the bottom of our hearts," Lauren says sincerely, though tears stream down her face. She and Michael hug Elvis.

Why from the bottom of their heart? What about the top?

CHAPTER THIRTY-SIX

GROWING THE
51 FAMILY

THE NEXT MORNING, ELVIS, ZANE, GERTIE, MINI-ELVIS, AND I laze around on picnic blankets in the center of town. School still hasn't reopened—we are waiting on a mass shipment of Lysol from Washington, DC, to neutralize the smell—and though the adults have left us a long list of chores to do while we're on vacation, we've been ignoring them. No one can yell at us; we just saved not only Area 51 but the whole state of Nevada.

Everyone—humans and Break Throughs—seems to be in a good mood and enjoying the beautiful weather. The Spotifies are playing ABBA, Chill is chilling in the sun, and the Retinayas are rocking custom-made sunglasses. Even Uncle Anish has taken off his uniform.

"What's going to happen to Ms. Spitz?" I ask, because even though she was willing to murder us all with a killer space toilet, I feel bad for her. Apparently,

she confessed to working with the Arthogus. They had offered her the one thing she wanted more than anything else: a trip to space.

It must be hard to want something so badly that you're willing to give up everything to get it. I also think about poor Ms. Moleratty having to say goodbye to Big Head, the love of her life, after the uprising, and never being able to talk to him again. How all she has left of him is that necklace and her memories.

I look over at Elvis, and my heart squeezes. As much as I'm pretending to be relaxed and enjoying the beautiful day, I'm devastated about our upcoming goodbye.

"Actually, she has a choice: she can either go to Galzoria with us this afternoon so their government can safely experiment on her and learn more about humans, or she can be sent to the Arthogus neighborhood with Belcher and Roidrage," Elvis says. He seems sad too. I'm not totally sure what he's feeling about returning to Galzoria—I've been too afraid to ask. Maybe he thinks that distant planet *could* feel like home after all. Maybe he'll let go of Area 51, his lilac house, his alien sheets, Lauren and Michael and Pickles. Me.

"Well, if she stays, she'll be doing yoga in no time," Zane says.

"And if she goes, she'll give Galzoria valuable intel on why humans have 'funny bones.' That's always seemed so weird to us," Mini-Elvis says. "Also, why is yawning contagious? And the belly button? Shouldn't that close up eventually?"

Later, when it comes time for the Galzoria to leave, I stand next to Zane and Gertie and smile, even though I desperately want to cry. It's time to say goodbye to my first and best friend.

Again, I think about how Break Throughs can have a very different understanding of time than humans. And now I get it, because I feel both like Elvis and I have just met and also like I've known him forever.

We gather in the spot where Elvis's family first arrived. Their ship is already hovering and ready to go.

"I oiled up the flux capacitor," Dino-Dad says. "And I've sanitized all touchable surfaces."

"Where is the map?" Dino-Mom says.

Elvis doesn't say anything, though the map is clearly in his mom's hands. He just looks at me, then Lauren, then Michael. Pickles lets out a loud, sad bark.

"I can't do this," Elvis says, at first quietly, then louder. "I can't do this!"

"Come on, everyone. I want to get back in time to watch the new *Nailed It: Multisensory Edition,*" Dino-Mom says, and tries to usher Elvis toward the ship.

"I'm sorry. I'm not going. I can't go," Elvis says.

"Son, this isn't a choice. You are Galzorian. You belong on Galzoria," Dino-Dad says.

"No. I belong in my home. And my home is here. With all these people." Elvis gestures to us. "They are my family too.

"I'm sorry, but I'm staying." Elvis is so calm and assertive it suddenly feels like he has the power to make it true. And I think he does. He's not going anywhere.

Don't forget about us!

I'm so relieved I could cry. Lauren actually does cry as she pulls Elvis into her arms and whispers something in his ear. I don't know what she says, but I imagine it's something like "I love you" or "Thank you" or "You're my home too."

Dino-Mom sighs through her nostrils, and her exhale is so heavy and loud I wonder if

230

flames will come out. And then I remember she is a dinosaur, not a dragon.

She looks at Lauren and then at Elvis. Her tiny hands tremble, as if they too want to reach out and grab Elvis. We wait with bated breath for her verdict.

"All right. If this is what you want," Dino-Mom says. Her voice is both sad and hopeful. "All I need is for you to be happy, Elvis. I'll be beaming love from Galzoria daily, like I always have."

Elvis nods, like he knows this, like he has always known this. I wonder if my parents are beaming love at me from somewhere. I decide there's no harm in believing they are.

"And hopefully, the Arthogus will try to attack again so we have an excuse to come visit," she says. Lauren clears her throat. "Or I don't hope that. Doesn't matter. We'll find a way back."

"I'm going to miss you, buddy," Elvis says, and crouches so he's eye to eye with his brother. "You're a cool little dude."

"That's because I'm just like you but smaller," Mini-Elvis says.

"Exactly," Elvis says, and he smiles, but I can tell from his glittery eyes that it's one of those brave smiles that hurt. I am sure all of this hurts. It can't be easy saying goodbye to his Galzorian family.

"Hey, Mom, Dad, can I stay here also?" Mini-Elvis asks suddenly.

"What?" Dino-Dad says distractedly, since he is digging around in his fanny pack for some hand wipes. I wonder if they are extra small.

"I want to stay. I can finish my field research here for my kindergarten PhD. It will be like how Galzoria sometimes go to Peeyou for a study-abroad program. I won't stay too long. Five or ten human years at most. You can come back to retrieve me then and visit Elvis," Mini-Elvis says. "The government will be okay with it if if I am gathering important research data."

"I don't know," Dino-Mom says. "Where would you live?"

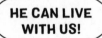

HE CAN LIVE WITH US!

Dino-Mom and Dino-Dad look at each other, deciding.

"You know how you taught me that family is the most important thing in the universe, and it literally grows our dimensions? Well, Elvis is also my family, and I want to spend more time with him. My project will be to see how we both grow from knowing each other," Mini-Elvis says.

"I want to grow from knowing him too," Elvis says, reaching out to hug his brother.

"Me too," I say, thinking about how much I've grown from knowing Elvis. How having him as a best friend is even more beautiful than a space parade.

"You are an Earthling with only three dimensions, but I appreciate the thought, Sky," Mini-Elvis says.

"Okay. But you can only stay for five human years. Ten tops," Dino-mom says.

"Can we please get this show on the road?" Ms. Spitz asks, her helmet off, and she sprays Dino-Dad so thoroughly with her spit that I wonder if there are enough wipes in the world for him to feel clean again.

"Don't worry. We'll put her in the cargo hold," Dino-Mom says to Dino-Dad, who turns to look at Elvis.

"Maybe when we come back we can visit for longer. Spend more time with you, Elvis," Dino-Dad says. "We spent this whole trip pretending to be sightseeing so we could keep an eye on you, son."

"That's what you were doing?" Elvis asks. "Why didn't you say so?"

"I'm sorry. Next time, we'll be more direct, like the Earthlings tend to be, and just ask to spend time with you."

"Oh, one rule, Mini-E. Stay away from Spike!" Dino-Mom says.

I don't want his allergies acting up.

We promise. We'll keep six feet apart!

You better stay MORE than six feet away!

Goodbye, Dino-Mom and Dino-Dad, I think as they make their way into their spaceship. *Thank you for letting me keep my home.*

CHAPTER THIRTY-SEVEN

NEVER A DULL MOMENT

AFTER THE GALZORIAN SHIP ZIPS UP INTO THE COSMOS, WE stand watching the sky together even though there is nothing left to see. Elvis's Dino-mom and dad and Ms. Spitz are gone, traveling through space and time back to Galzoria.

Come in, Agent Patel! Come in, stat!

"What's going on?" Elvis asks. We turn to see my uncle on his feet, frantically pacing and yelling into his walkie-talkie.

"What? No! That isn't possible!" he yells, bending over as if in pain. My stomach knots in fear. I rarely see Uncle Anish panicked. This must be serious.

Never a dull moment in Area 51, I think.

Uncle Anish takes his walkie and tucks it onto his belt loop.

"I'm so sorry, but I have to go," he tells us, since we're all staring at him with concern.

"Uncle Anish, are you okay?" I ask.

"Sky, I don't know how to tell you this," he says. Now I'm straight-up terrified. Did something happen to the Galzoria? Was there a problem with liftoff?

"Are my parents okay?" Mini-Elvis asks, clutching his blanket. Lauren pulls him closer, as if to protect him.

He's so smart I sometimes forget he's only five.

"They're fine," Uncle Anish says.

"Is it Grandma? Is she all right? Is she healthy?" I ask. I've been so preoccupied with keeping us all alive here and thinking about losing my best friend, it never occurred to me that my grandma could be hurt or sick somewhere else.

"Yes. She's okay. I mean, sort of," Uncle Anish says. "She's been . . . well, she's been taken hostage at the other base, Area 52."

SORT OF?!?!?!

"What are you talking about?" I ask, and almost laugh. Grandma is supposed to be living at a retirement home in the center of our old town. In California. She can't be in Area 52. "She's at the only other alien portal on Earth?"

Grandma doesn't even know Area 51 exists.

There is no way she could have found herself in Area 52.

It doesn't make sense.

"That can't be," I say. My knees are shaking, and I feel Elvis wrap his arm around me to hold me up. Mini-Elvis grabs my hand.

"I promise she'll be fine," Uncle Anish says. "We'll rescue her."

"Why would anyone want to kidnap my grandma?" I ask, incredulous and scared.

"Don't worry, she can take care of herself," Uncle Anish says.

She's trained in all the martial arts. She's been an undercover FBAI agent for five decades!

WAIT, WHAT?!?! GRANDMA IS AN FBAI AGENT?!?

BELCHER AND ROIDRAGE'S RETINAYA EYEBALL COOKIES

INGREDIENTS

2-1/4 cups all-purpose flour

I teaspoon baking soda

1/2 teaspoon salt

3/4 cup butter (soft)

1/2 cup granulated sugar

1/2 cup brown sugar

I tablespoon vanilla

2 eggs (preferably from Egglandia, but Earth chicken eggs will do just fine)

I cup Retinaya eyeball blood vessels (if unavailable, replace with I cup Fruity Pebbles cereal)

INSTRUCTIONS

1. Turn on the old oven to 350° F. (I guess a new oven will work too.)

2. Make your cookie sheet less sticky by either covering it with parchment paper or spraying it with cooking spray (which will make it MORE sticky now, but less sticky later.)

3. In a bowl, mix the flour, baking soda, and salt. While mixing, dance to one whole song. (I prefer to use a song by Sir Mix-a-Lot, but you do you, my friend.) Set this bowl aside.

4. In a stand mixer (or with an electric mixer), beat your butter and sugars. When I say beat,

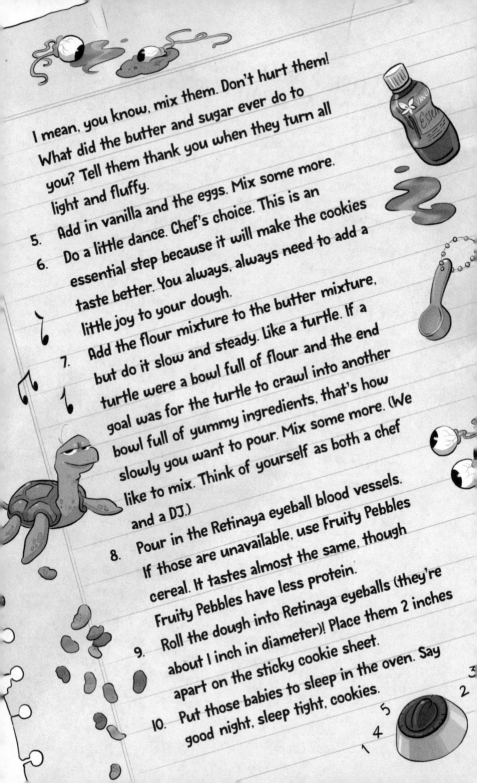

I mean, you know, mix them. Don't hurt them! What did the butter and sugar ever do to you? Tell them thank you when they turn all light and fluffy.

5. Add in vanilla and the eggs. Mix some more.

6. Do a little dance. Chef's choice. This is an essential step because it will make the cookies taste better. You always, always need to add a little joy to your dough.

7. Add the flour mixture to the butter mixture, but do it slow and steady. Like a turtle. If a turtle were a bowl full of flour and the end goal was for the turtle to crawl into another bowl full of yummy ingredients, that's how slowly you want to pour. Mix some more. (We like to mix. Think of yourself as both a chef and a DJ.)

8. Pour in the Retinaya eyeball blood vessels. If those are unavailable, use Fruity Pebbles cereal. It tastes almost the same, though Fruity Pebbles have less protein.

9. Roll the dough into Retinaya eyeballs (they're about 1 inch in diameter)! Place them 2 inches apart on the sticky cookie sheet.

10. Put those babies to sleep in the oven. Say good night, sleep tight, cookies.

11. Bake for 10 minutes, until they look like . . . well . . . cooked cookies.

12. Let them chill out for a bit. You chill out too. Maybe take a walk around the block.

13. Next, clean up your kitchen. Yup, even that blob that dropped on the floor. Believe me, it's there.

14. EAT THE COOKIES. TASTE THAT JOY. NOM NOM NOM.

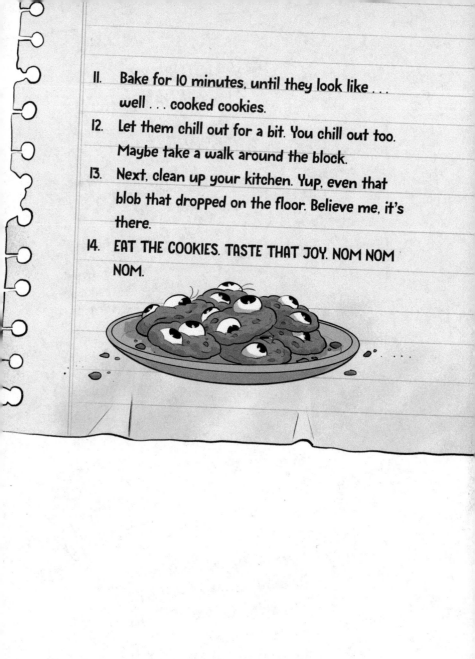

NELL LEGSWOLE'S
INTERSTELLAR BANANA BREAD

INGREDIENTS

2 bananas (preferably old sad soft spotted ones that no one wants to eat)

2-1/2 cups flour

1 tablespoon baking powder

1/4 teaspoon salt

1 cup milk (preferably from Planet Dairyian, but if not available, then from a cow)

1/4 cup melted butter (compliment it so it gets extra soft)

1 cup granulated sugar

2 eggs (preferably from Egglandia, but Earth chicken eggs make for a decent substitute)

3 full-size Milky Way bars, chopped (never a bad idea to buy a fourth for dessert or for emergencies)

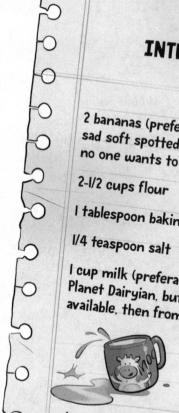

INSTRUCTIONS

1. Set the oven to 350° F, which is ten degrees less than 360°, which is a full circle. Don't turn in a full circle. You will get dizzy. Just, you know, turn on the oven.

2. Spray the loaf pan with cooking spray or grease it with butter so your Interstellar Banana Bread doesn't stick. We want this to come out like a rectangle, people!

3. Combine the flour, baking powder, and salt in a

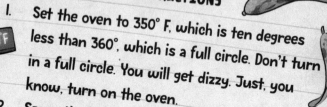

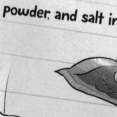

large mixing bowl, and mix until you just have a bowl of white powdery stuff.

4. In a different bowl, mix the sugar and melted butter using either a stand mixer or a hand mixer. Kindly remind the sugar and butter that they need to get along. We want this banana bread to taste peaceful.

5. Crack the two eggs into the bowl with the sugar-and-melted-butter combo. DO NOT, I REPEAT, DO NOT PUT THE SHELLS IN THE BOWL. Those go in the garbage or compost. I tried cooking with them once and I cracked a tooth.

6. Add half a cup of milk and half of the flour mixture to the sugar/butter/eggs concoction. Mix to ten rounds of the "Y.M.C.A." chorus.

7. Repeat step 6 with the rest of the milk and flour.

8. Add in the sad spotted bananas. Thank them for their service and then mix those babies up.

9. Add the chopped Milky Way bars, mix, and make a wish on a star. (If you are baking during the day and you cannot see stars, don't worry. Make a wish anyway. They are still out there. We want to get that wish baked into the bread.)

10. Pour the batter into your loaf pan. Tell it to stay rectangular. (Don't worry. It will listen. Banana bread is very obedient.)

11. Cook for 1 hour and 15 minutes, give or take 15 minutes. What? This isn't a science! I don't know how obedient your bread is and how well your eggs and sugar are getting along. Maybe your bread needs a little extra time in its sauna. Maybe it gets hot easily. Whatever. Take it out when it's ready.

12. Let it cool in the pan. You don't want hot and sweaty post-sauna banana bread.

13. Clean your kitchen so well that if you drop some banana bread on the floor, you can follow the five-second rule without it being gross.

14. Eat! Share! But make sure to save a piece for tomorrow's breakfast. Tell your parents its bread. (Know in your heart it's really cake.)

ACKNOWLEDGMENTS

Thank you so much to Hannah Hill and the rest of the amazing Delacorte Press/Random House Children's team. I'm so thankful to every single one of you who had a hand in shepherding this book to publication. Thank you so much to my agent extraordinaire, Jennifer Joel. A giant thank you to Lavanya Naidu, without whom this book wouldn't be nearly as much fun or beautiful. Forever thank you to Elaine Koster and Susan Kamil.

Hugely grateful to my writer village. Special thanks to Charlotte Huang, Kayla Cagan, and Amy Spalding, who are always down for brainstorming. Huge shout-out to Adele Griffin for her endless generosity. Thank you to Rose Brock, Max Brallier, Stuart Gibbs, Gordon Korman, Sarah Mlynowski, James Ponti, Melissa Posten, Aly Gerber, and Christina Soontornvat for their middle-grade wisdom and for making me laugh on the daily. And thank you to my oldest and closest friends and family for always being there for me. You know who you are.

This book was improved immeasurably by my

two kiddos, Elili and Luca, and I am eternally grateful for the help. If you're ever looking for an editor, you should hire Elili while she's still cheap. And while I'm talking about my kids, just wanted to put in print how proud I am to be their mommy. Final thank you to Indy Flore, my co-captain and partner in crime.

© INDY FLORE

UFO:
Unidentified
Food Object

JULIE BUXBAUM is the *New York Times* bestselling author of the young adult novels *Tell Me Three Things*, *What to Say Next*, *Hope and Other Punch Lines*, *Admission*, and *Year on Fire*. She also wrote the critically acclaimed *The Opposite of Love* and *After You*. She lives in Los Angeles with her husband and two children.

JULIEBUXBAUM.COM

satyam agarwala

LAVANYA NAIDU is a children's book illustrator, animator, and director from Kolkata, India. Over the last decade she has illustrated numerous children's books while also working on multiple animation productions for television and film. Lavanya now lives in Melbourne, Australia, with her husband and their ever-growing collection of plants.

@Lavanyanaidu